RESCUE MY HEART

Kate Sheffield is running an animal rescue centre when she meets gorgeous new vet Callan Jamieson. Kate's family is in crisis after the death of her father, and she is desperately trying to solve their problems while coping with her own grief. The rescue centre is also receiving threatening letters. Kate, convinced she can handle all this by herself, is reluctant to trust Callan after being hurt before by love. Can Callan rescue her heart?

Books by Carol MacLean
in the Linford Romance Library:

WILD FOR LOVE

CAROL MacLEAN

RESCUE MY HEART

Complete and Unabridged

LINFORD
Leicester

First published in Great Britain in 2011

First Linford Edition
published 2012

British Library CIP Data

MacLean, Carol.
    Rescue my heart. - -
    (Linford romance library)
    1. Love stories- -Fiction.
    2. Large type books.
    I. Title II. Series
    823.9'2–dc23

    ISBN 978–1–4448–1071–4

Published by
F. A. Thorpe (Publishing)
Anstey, Leicestershire

Set by Words & Graphics Ltd.
Anstey, Leicestershire
Printed and bound in Great Britain by
T. J. International Ltd., Padstow, Cornwall

This book is printed on acid-free paper

1

Kate Sheffield had just collided with the goat when the telephone rang. Gilly Goat bleated reproachfully and clattered across the kitchen tiles to the lush green grass in the walled garden outside. Kate rubbed her elbow where it had connected painfully with the floor.

'If you've eaten your new tether, there'll be trouble,' she called grimly to the goat while picking up Bob and Prickles who had wandered across from their box by the fire. They both suddenly rolled themselves protectively, snuffling and clicking their teeth.

'I'll get you a bowl of cat food in a moment,' she promised, putting the two tiny hedgehogs gently back into the cardboard box. The phone was still ringing insistently. Kate sighed, pushed her fair hair back from her face and hurried to the hall where the telephone sat on an elegant side table.

'Kate, darling, what took you so long?'

It was her mother. Kate prepared herself for the usual conversation.

'I thought you had had an accident and couldn't get to the phone. I really don't think it's safe for a young girl to live alone in the wilds like you do. Anything could happen and if it did, how would you get help? I do worry so about you, my love.'

'Firstly, Mum, I'm hardly a young girl. I'm thirty-one and quite capable of looking after myself. And secondly, Invermalloch House is hardly in the wilds. I'm a couple of miles from the village itself and I have Mrs Bennett on one side as a neighbour and the Connaughies on the other.'

'I do wish Gran hadn't gone and left her house to you. You'd still be here in Glasgow and I could easily pop in to see you like we used to do,' Mrs Sheffield said wistfully.

Kate felt a twinge of guilt and

sadness. Her mother sounded so lonely.

'I love it here, Mum,' she said softly, 'I really do. Argyllshire is beautiful with the sea so close and the woodlands and glens. You should see the colours now that autumn's here. Besides it's only two hours' drive from Glasgow to see you. That's okay.'

'Don't you miss the city at all?'

Kate thought of the hustle and bustle in the grey city streets, the smell of petrol fumes and the noise of the traffic.

'Honestly, no. I can't imagine ever returning to being a school librarian.'

'But you can't stay there forever. You must think of a career soon.'

'I'm settled at Invermalloch. Something will turn up when I'm ready.'

'If your dad was here . . . ' Mrs Sheffield's voice trailed off helplessly.

Kate felt a pain in her heart so intense it was physical. Her beloved father had died the previous winter, nine months before, and all the family were still reeling from the unexpectedness of his passing.

'I miss him too, Mum. We all do. Look, I'll come and see you soon. We'll go for a nice lunch in town and have a chat. What do you say?'

'Can you come tomorrow? I'm worried about Josh. I haven't heard from him in a month. I do wonder whether he might be trying to punish me in some way for Dad's death.'

No, thought Kate savagely, *he's simply a selfish immature guy who can't see beyond his own grief to everyone else's.*

But to her mother she said comfortingly, 'I'm sure he'll call soon. Josh was never one to keep good time. In fact I don't think I've ever even seen him wear a watch.'

'Maybe you're right. I want you to speak to Jenny for me, too. She's talking about quitting college. She won't listen to me but you know she always takes your advice.'

Jenny was Kate's youngest sibling and, at twenty-one, still treated as the baby of the family. This translated over the years into a lot of leeway and spoiling from Kate, Josh and Melissa. The four Sheffields had always been close as children and teenagers but since last winter Kate had the impression that the ties were loosening, slipping apart like silk ribbons. It was up to her to tie them back together tightly, since her poor mother was incapable, wrapped in her own sorrow as she was.

'I'll come tomorrow, then,' Kate promised. She let her mother talk about her sore back and her hospital appointments to have her heart monitored and her friends' various ailments. The conversation washed over her in its familiarity. It was a daily occurrence. Mrs Sheffield's health absorbed her.

Kate doubted her mother was anything but as strong as an ox, but she kept quiet. She rang off eventually with the firmly repeated promise that she would go down to Glasgow the next day.

The house was strangely quiet. Kate

could hear the breeze blowing outside. It rattled in the old house's chimneys and made the fire in the kitchen grate spark and splutter. The hazel tree screeched as its branches moved against the window pane of the games room. She made a mental note to prune it back since it was a decidedly sinister noise.

Looking beyond its gnarly boughs, Kate saw the rough grassy fields which gave way to willow scrub and then dense woodland. The woods shone copper, burgundy and ochre as the leaves turned, leading them into the darkness of another autumn and winter. Kate shivered and wrapped her arms around herself. Suddenly she wished she was down in the city, having lunch at her mother's house with Mum, Jenny and Melissa.

If only Josh would come home from London to complete the picture. If indeed he was still there, busking and living in a squat in Hackney. Was it possible he had moved on? Was that why he hadn't written or called? He was twenty-five, Kate reminded herself; old enough to look out for himself. But London was a huge place and tended to be unforgiving to those without money or ties.

To distract herself, she went to check on the foxes. They had the run of the living room and they barked a welcome as she pushed the door open. Really, it was time for them to be released. Freddy's foot had healed nicely and Loxy's fur seemed free of mange now. Kate decided she would get the vet to give them a last check-up soon, and then she'd take them back to the woods and release them.

The letter box slammed and she froze, her heart thumping fast. She made herself breathe more easily as she went to the hall and stared. On the mat at the front door lay two envelopes. She heard the postman whistling and the clang of the front gate as he followed his route to the Connaughies and then back to Invermalloch village.

One envelope was ruby red. It looked just as if it would contain a party invitation or a celebration card. The other was a long, thin rectangle, mustard-coloured. Kate knew perfectly well what it held. She felt sick as she inched round it and picked up the red envelope. The other could wait; she couldn't bear to open it now.

The red one was indeed a party invitation, from Melissa. The party was to be held in a trendy club in the centre of Glasgow to celebrate Melissa's friend Amy's thirtieth birthday. It was in a week's time and was addressed to 'Kate and partner'. She sighed. Was it worse to stomach an evening of loud music and flashing lights on her own, or to feel the guilt of inflicting it on a friend also? Besides, who would she ask?

An image of Matthew flitted across her memory. She pushed it down. It only made her think of Moyra and that wouldn't do. Not now with that . . . that *thing* sitting on the mat. No stamp, she noticed. Just like the last one.

There was a sudden sharp rapping at the door. Kate jumped. Opening it carefully, she saw a small boy with tousled hair and grass-stained trousers.

'Miss, miss can you come, please? You need to rescue this big bird — it's all torn up in wire! This is the animal rescue place, isn't it?'

'Yes, it is. People usually bring sick or injured wildlife to me, but I can come to it, of course I can.' Kate quickly grabbed her warm jacket and hurried after the small boy.

They ran down the lane, across the trickling burn and up another lane, finally arriving at a dark, stone house set back against a small hillside.

'Oh, you're David Connaughie,' panted Kate as she stopped at the entrance and tried to catch her breath.

'Yes, that's me. Come on. Hurry!'

They rushed round the side of the house, Kate wishing she was ten again and filled with boundless energy. David came to a halt. Kate did likewise. Mrs

Connaughie stood, arms folded, lips pursed, watching a man struggle to subdue a terrified herring gull stuck in the wire fence. It was pecking viciously at him with its sharp beak.

Kate's first impression of him was of darkness. He was a tall, thin man with jet-black hair, a shadowed jaw that no amount of shaving would lighten, and tanned face and arms. Not the tan of an expensive holiday, but the weathered skin of someone who spent considerable time out of doors. He glanced up briefly and Kate glimpsed brown eyes so deep in colour that they were hardly distinguishable from their black pupils.

She flushed and looked away but he was already back to his task, his long fingers gently pulling wire strands away from the bird's leg.

'David, what did you fetch her for?' said Mrs Connaughie sharply. 'The vet's here now, he can handle it.'

Kate flushed again, this time in anger. The few times she had met Mrs

Connaughie the woman had either ignored her if possible or been abrupt to the point of rudeness. Kate had no idea why. She could only imagine that the Connaughies did not like incomers to the village.

'That's not the vet,' Kate said now. She could hear the challenge in her own voice but, too late, the words were out. They hung in the air while Mrs Connaughie glared and David's mouth made an 'oh' of surprise.

Then the dark man chuckled. He held the newly freed gull firmly and extended his hand to Kate.

'Actually, I am the vet. Sorry to disappoint you. I'm Callan Jamieson.' His voice had a soft, irish lilt like melting butter.

'I . . . I'm not disappointed,' Kate said foolishly. She kicked herself mentally and added, 'But where's Morris? I only saw him last week.'

Morris Calvin, the village vet, had been up to Invermalloch House to immunise the foxes against distemper.

He hadn't mentioned going away.

'Mr Calvin had to visit his son in Dubai at short notice about family matters. He'll be gone for six months so I'm the locum vet in the meantime. I hope that suits you.'

Kate took the gull from him expertly. 'I can fix his leg. It'll save you the bother.' Now she was being as abrupt with him as Mrs Connaughie was with her. He had unsettled her, with his dark good looks and rich voice.

Like the gull, she wanted to fly from here. She grasped the bird tightly and headed for Invermalloch House where she could bind its leg and cage it until it was ready for release.

His voice followed her down the path. 'I'll come by tomorrow, see how the patient is doing.'

It was the evening before Kate touched the envelope on the mat. The herring gull was safely caged, its leg disinfected and bandaged. She drew the curtains against the early dusk and lit a fire in the living room hearth. Slowly she tore open the envelope. A single piece of paper slid out. She turned it over, knowing already what to expect.

In bold capital lettering it said, *I WARNED YOU.*

2

Callan Jamieson whistled as he locked the veterinary surgery door. It was a beautiful, crisp October day. The sky was an intense powder blue, the sun was shining and the rowan berries were bright red on the trees. It was the kind of day that lifts the spirits.

It was more than that, though — he felt as if he might feel this happy for the rest of his life. He conjured up an image from the day before; saw again Kate Sheffield's willowy figure with her determined face and unruly fair hair. She had dealt so calmly and competently with the injured gull, and he had been impressed. It was not something he could ever imagine Annette coping with in a million years. Perhaps that was unfair — Kate clearly had a way with animals and it was her job. Annette, on the other hand, was . . . well, a different personality type altogether.

He shut that particular door in his mind. It was old history and not something he wanted to revisit. No, much better to anticipate seeing Kate again. Was it love at first sight? Callan chuckled to himself as he drove the car along the narrow village streets and out into the glen. Could love have finally hit him at the relatively late age of thirty-five? Well, if it wasn't love, it felt very close to it. The fact was, he couldn't wait to see her again.

He parked the car at the bottom of the lane, swung his bag carelessly onto his shoulder and sauntered up to Invermalloch House, feeling the sun soak warmly into his back.

Kate was in the front garden holding a goat by the horns. Callan was struck afresh by her slenderness. Her blonde hair was escaping from a pony tail and curled free around her face and, as she turned towards him, he saw that her eyes were grey — slate grey like a stormy sea. She wasn't conventionally pretty, he decided, but the combination of those eyes fringed by black lashes, her high cheekbones and generous mouth made his heart beat just a little faster.

'Mr Jamieson.' She nodded. The goat pulled but she held it firmly.

'Callan,' he said easily as he opened the gate to join her on the front lawn. 'Can I help you there?'

'No, no,' Kate said politely, 'It's just Gilly Goat. She's escaped her tether again and this time she's helped herself to the shrubbery . . . nibbled all the tops of the plants.'

As she spoke she was leading the recalcitrant goat towards the back walled garden. Callan followed them.

The walled garden was a kitchen garden and there were remains of the season's crops. A huge rhubarb plant dominated one corner and there were some stems showing that a couple of rows of potatoes were waiting to be dug up. Kate tied the Gilly to a post where the goat could graze without reaching the crops. Callan hunkered down and frowned. The original tether rope lay there. He fingered the end of it thoughtfully.

'What . . . ?' he began, then saw the set of Kate's jaw. Her eyes were shuttered, so he let it go for the moment.

'Would you like a cup of tea while you examine the patient?' Kate asked. Her face was hidden from him as she led the way into the large kitchen. There was a roaring fire in the old hearth and an ancient, faded blue easy chair was drawn up to it. Callan saw a book, page down on the arm of the chair. A solid but battered looking table took up most of the centre of the kitchen, with the cupboards, sink and cast iron Aga seemingly crammed into a jumbled corner. He took in an image of dried flowers, garlic strings, jars of pasta shapes and a row of ceramic jugs all different sizes and patterns. The overall effect was one of welcome and casual comfort — a real living space.

As if she read his thoughts, Kate said

'Sorry, it's a bit messy. I spend a lot of time in here. It reminds me of my Gran.'

'So this is your Gran's home?'

'Yes, she left it to me, along with the rescue centre work. I've been here about four months now.'

'I'm so sorry for your loss.'

Kate looked startled, then a slow smile relaxed her features. 'It's okay. My grandmother is still very much alive. She was simply finding it all too much to maintain, so she gave it to me and now has a wonderful, modern sheltered housing flat in Glasgow.'

'Well I'm sure she's very proud of what you are doing here. You've done a fine job on this chap's leg.'

Callan was looking approvingly at the recuperating gull whose cage Kate had now brought into the room. He examined the bird more closely, taking his time and enjoying the background sounds of the kettle singing and cups and saucers clinking as Kate made the tea.

18

'What do you think?' Kate's soft voice shook him from his reverie. 'Have I done enough to save the leg?'

Callan looked at her warmly. 'You really care, don't you?'

Kate was surprised. 'Of course, it's my job.'

'Working with animals is never just a job.'

Now it was Kate's turn to look at him, warmth in her tone. 'You're right. Each patient is a worry to me until they are back on their two feet — or four!'

There was a moment of perfect understanding between them as they smiled at one another. Looking back, Callan pinpointed that moment as the start of his friendship with Kate Sheffield.

The shrill call of the telephone instantly broke the mood. It switched to loudspeaker as Kate answered the call, so Callan could not help overhearing the conversation.

'Hi, Kate, it's Melissa, here. Did you get my card about Amy's party?'

Kate picked up slowly. 'Hello, Liss. Yes I got it, thanks. Not sure if . . . '

'Don't bother to think of an excuse. Just come along. It'll be a blast. Plus Amy's looking forward to meeting you again. And bring a date. Aren't there any gorgeous single men in Invermalloch?'

Callan could see Kate flush as she gripped the receiver. 'Look, I'll come for a short while to celebrate with Amy, but it's not my scene, Liss, you know that. I'll see you next week. We'll catch up, I promise. Love you.'

Kate put the phone down firmly. She sighed.

'Big sister?' Callan asked, grinning.

'Sounds like it since she's so bossy, but no, Melissa's younger than me, but an awful lot more confident,' said Kate smiling ruefully. 'She's a complete party animal, very sociable and bubbly.'

Callan had a sudden, brilliant idea and the words were out of his mouth before his brain could filter it. 'May I escort you to Amy's party?'

Kate opened and shut her mouth. Her grey eyes narrowed. 'It's very kind of you, I'm sure,' she said stiffly, 'But not necessary, I assure you.'

'I'm sorry,' Callan said quickly. 'Of course you already have a date in mind. It was presumptuous of me.' He waited, watching in veiled amusement as she suddenly found the pattern on her teacup fascinating.

There was a long pause. Then Kate spoke quietly. 'Actually I don't . . . have someone in mind, I mean.'

'Well then. I'm a very good dancer, I have all my own teeth and am well versed in polite party chit-chat, so what do you say?'

'Very well, then, but I only hope you don't find me too dull. I don't dance and I don't drink.'

Callan picked up his bag and gave a mock bow. 'Until next week, then. I shall look forward to it.'

Kate still looked a bit stunned as she showed him out. He waved as he locked the gate behind him and set off down the lane to his car.

Kate Sheffield was a puzzle, all right. She was gorgeous but didn't seem to know it. She could mend a bird's broken leg beautifully but couldn't dance. And there was mystery surrounding her, too. The goat's tether had not been chewed; it had been cut clean through. Someone had deliberately let the goat loose to damage the garden, but Kate had not wanted him to know that. What was going on, Callan had no idea, but he was determined to find out more about Kate whether she wanted him to or not.

3

'Betty Ruskin keeps pestering me to join the ramblers. At my age! Why on earth would I want to go out in the cold, wet, windy weather walking through muddy fields with all these get-fit fanatics, I ask you? It's all very well Betty saying she enjoys it, but she hasn't got a bad leg like I have, has she? Or heart palpitations.'

Kate stopped scrubbing potatoes and gave her mother a look. 'Mum, you should go. You and Dad used to love country walks. It might actually do your leg and your heart some good.'

It was a week later and Kate had finally managed to make the two-hour trip to Glasgow. Severe autumn gales had toppled the top of the living room chimney at Invermalloch House and dislodged a few roof slates too. It had taken time to organise a roofer to come and fix the damage, particularly as the entire village had suffered from the stormy weather. It seemed there were ladders and white vans everywhere as people rushed to secure their houses before the winter.

Then she had been worried about Gilly the goat, who was not herself. Kate suspected Gilly had eaten a plant that had disagreed with her, but couldn't find anything out of the ordinary within range of the goat's tether.

An uneasiness sat in the pit of her stomach as she examined Gilly. What if . . . what if the same person who had cut the tether had decided to work more wickedness? Would someone be cruel enough to poison the goat? And why was this someone so determined that Kate and the animal rescue centre should go? At least there had been no more threatening letters.

'Your Dad did enjoy a stroll,' Mrs Sheffield was saying softly. 'I know it's kind of Betty to invite me to come along, but I can't bear the idea of going without him.' She wiped her eyes.

'Oh, Mum,' said Kate, giving her a long hug. 'I know it's hard, but please say you'll consider going with Betty. I hate to think of you here being lonely.'

Her mother sniffed a little and gave a weak smile. 'I'm not lonely. I've got Jenny for company. Mind you she has her own life to lead, I suppose, and I mustn't keep her back.'

'Which reminds me — she'll be here soon and expecting some lunch,' Kate answered lightly. She returned to preparing the potatoes and missed her mother's fleeting, worried frown.

★ ★ ★

The chicken was roasted to perfection, the potatoes were crisp and crunchy on the outside and fluffy inside and the french beans steamed just right. So why was Jenny not eating, Kate wondered? Her younger sister had arrived back from tennis amid a clatter of rackets, trainers and books. All these were left to fall where they landed on the hall floor as Jenny ran upstairs two at a time to change, calling a casual greeting as she went.

Now that she was sitting at the dining room table opposite, toying with her food, Kate had a chance to examine her. It had been four months since she had last seen her baby sister and she was shocked at how much weight Jenny had lost. Her face had lost its soft prettiness now that her cheekbones were prominent. Her once curvy figure had vanished and her upper arms looked painfully thin.

Jenny appeared oblivious and chattered on about tennis and jogging and Pilates while her mother slipped more chicken onto her already full plate.

'Mum tells me you're thinking of quitting college,' said Kate rather bluntly. She couldn't think how to approach the subject otherwise.

'Not forever.' Jenny cut some beans into smaller pieces, but didn't eat any.

'But Heidi's asked me to go with her. You know she's signed up to a sponsored cycle across India.'

Mrs Sheffield dropped a spoon; it clattered loudly in the sudden silence. Then they were all speaking at once — Kate saying there was no way Jenny should give up her degree for that, Jenny shouting that it was her life, not Kate's, and Mrs Sheffield asking repeatedly when on earth her niece Heidi had come up with such a hare-brained scheme and how could her sister Hilda allow it to happen?

'I'm going and that's that,' Jenny said fiercely before storming out of the room. Kate and her mother stared at each other and then at Jenny's plate of chicken, potatoes and beans, which had been stirred and mixed and chopped, but not eaten — not a single bite.

'Mum, what have you been keeping from me? How long has this been going on? She's as thin as a stick.'

'I thought it was a phase, her not eating properly; part of mourning for her dad, that it would quickly stop, but she's not getting any better and she's exercising all the time.'

Kate rose to go upstairs, where they could hear the thump of rock music.

Mrs Sheffield put out a hand to stop her and shook her head. 'Leave her, please, Kate. She's angry. Let her cool down a bit first and then maybe you can reason with her. She won't listen to me. I thought she hated college. But now she wants to cycle goodness knows where for months. I'm losing her — just as I've lost Josh.'

'Has he phoned?'

'No, but he sent a postcard. It has a London scene and postmark, so he must still be there.'

Kate brewed a pot of coffee, glad of a distraction, a comforting routine when all around her was disintegrating. Somehow she would have to find a way to persuade Jenny to stay at college and eat healthily . . . find Josh and get him to come home . . . encourage her mother to get out and make a new life for herself . . .

Unexpectedly she thought of Callan Jamieson. He had charmed her into agreeing to go out with him tonight. He had a deep chuckle that she liked. But more than that, when he had spoken about his work — and hers — there was a solid sincerity about the man that was very appealing. Solid was good. Everything else in Kate's life was scattering and chaotic like autumn leaves blown by a capricious wind.

'I saw Moyra in the shops this morning,' Mrs Sheffield said, glancing sideways at Kate as she poured a mug of coffee. 'She asked after you.'

Kate bit down hard on her lip; her hands shook as she took the milk jug.

'You have to forgive and move on,' her mother said gently, moving the jug away, 'It's been three years now.'

Kate shook her head bitterly. 'Some things just cannot be forgiven. Was Matthew with her?'

It was strange, but it still hurt more

that Moyra had betrayed her than that Matthew had. He was a man, after all — wasn't it to be expected that he would be tempted by another woman, even if he was engaged to Kate and two weeks away from his church vows?

But Moyra . . . she and Kate had been best friends since the first day of primary school. They had shared giggles, sleepovers, swim parties and all the rest of a happy childhood. They had gone to the same high school and kept their close friendship going despite attending different colleges. Of course that meant that when Kate met Matthew, it was inevitable that Moyra should meet him too. They had all got on well and Kate was pleased that her two favourite people enjoyed each other's company around her.

At that time Moyra suddenly acquired a boyfriend, Jimmy, who hung out with them too, but always seemed that little bit further out of the circle. Kate and Matthew were engaged for two years then, just before the wedding, he and Moyra disappeared, leaving Kate a phone message.

They were deeply sorry, they had said; they couldn't help themselves any more. They had hidden their love for too long. Please forgive them. They would see her soon and explain.

Her parents had both urged Kate to meet Matthew and Moyra, to confront what they had done and to move on from it. But Kate had set her jaw firmly, frozen any mention of the pair with her large, grey eyes and gone on with her life. But there were no more boyfriends, no more close friendships. Just Kate and her family and her job.

They cleared the table together, both lost in their own thoughts. A door slammed — Jenny had gone out, avoiding them.

'I have to talk to her,' Kate said, looking out the big, bay window onto the street where she could see Jenny jogging fast, her blonde ponytail swinging and her legs kicking high.

'She's always worshipped you,' agreed her mother. 'But now . . . well, she doesn't want to take any advice.'

'I'll invite her up to Invermalloch. Perhaps up there it will give us time to sort things through.'

★   ★   ★

The afternoon passed comfortably enough. Kate helped her mother tidy and clean the spare bedroom between plenty of cups of tea and chats. She could sense her mother relaxing as the day wore on, reminiscing about times she and Mr Sheffield had had as a young couple and as parents to their growing family. The stories were warm, funny and loving.

Kate was surprised when the doorbell rang. 'It can't be time already! I haven't showered or changed yet!'

Callan Jamieson was dressed in dark, casual trousers and jacket under which was a cobalt blue shirt that brought out his dark good looks. He handed Kate a sprig of sweet-smelling freesias with a grin.

'You look lovely, Miss Sheffield.'

'You're teasing me, Mr Jamieson,' Kate said coolly, but her grey eyes were warm as she introduced him to her mother. 'Give me half an hour and I'll be ready.'

She was as good as her word. Gone were the faded jeans and T-shirt, the blonde hair piled into a rough ponytail and the smut of dust on her left cheek. Instead Kate's hair was shining and hanging loose to her shoulders. She wore a pale turquoise top over silk trousers and high heels. A tiny sequinned clutch bag completed her look.

Maybe it was called a clutch bag because that's what you did as you waited nervously to go to a party you didn't want to go to, with a man you didn't really know, thought Kate as she gripped the bag tightly.

For a moment Callan didn't speak. He just stared. Then with a clearing of his throat, he said gruffly, 'Very nice. Off to the ball, then.'

★ ★ ★

Amy's thirtieth birthday party was being celebrated at Denham's, a night-club off Sauchiehall Street. Glasgow was buzzing with the usual mob of Saturday night revellers and party-goers. Kate and Callan pushed their way politely through the crowds until they found the club entrance.

Amy had hired a private function suite; a huge room with a massive wooden dance floor. The tables surrounding it were cast in gloom but a brightly lit bar was already serving a steady queue.

'Kate!' A voice cut through the pulsing music.

They turned to see a tall girl bearing down on them with drinks in both hands. She was almost Kate's double, but where Kate was slender and angular, Melissa was curvy and round.

Her hair was a riot of carefully tended curls and she looked ready to spill out of her tight, ruby-red dress.

'Whoops!' she screamed happily. 'Nearly lost my heel there — six inches, they are! And who is this? My, Kate, you minx, you never said Invermalloch was full of gorgeous men — I must visit you sometime. Here's a vodka martini — oh, forgot, you don't drink . . . give it to your man here. Oh, there's Amy!'

And so she tottered off on her dangerously high heels, leaving Kate and Callan speechless.

'That's Melissa. My sister as you've gathered. She likes to party but she's not usually so merry at this early stage of the evening.'

'I'm sure she can take care of herself,' Callan said reassuringly, 'Now can I get you a soft drink?'

He guided her over to an empty table. Kate watched him weave amongst the dancers to get to the bar. She felt safe with him. It was an odd sensation and part of her — most of her — was fighting it. She couldn't let her guard down; at the end of the day she could only really trust herself.

Still, she felt that strange little lift of her mood when he returned with a fresh orange juice for her and a bottle of beer for himself.

'Tell me about yourself,' Kate said quickly. She sensed Callan had been about to ask the same question and was glad to get there first. She could hide safely in the shadows and listen to him talk.

He raised an eyebrow and grinned wryly as if he knew exactly why she was asking. 'Not a lot to tell,' he said. 'I'm a vet, as you know. An old friend of Morris Calvin's from college days. Poor Morris had to find cover quickly and thought of me. He knew I wanted away from Ireland for a bit.'

'May I ask why? Ireland is so beautiful.'

He hesitated. 'I have a cottage on the beach at Connemara, and you're right, Kate — it is beautiful and I miss it. But

I needed a break for . . . certain reasons. So here I am in bonny Scotland for six months.'

'And after that?'

'Who knows. Morris is looking for a partner in the practice. He's trying to entice me to stay. Now I've met you, maybe I will.'

Kate stiffened. She took a sip of her orange juice. Her grey eyes were cool as she looked at him. 'You hardly know me, Callan.'

'I know enough to say you are a very attractive woman and that I'm enjoying your company very much. No — don't draw away from me, Kate. I'm a gentleman and very trustworthy. Honestly.'

He chuckled. It was that deep, rumbling chuckle she found so engaging and suddenly she was smiling back at him too.

'That's better. Your eyes light up when you smile. Come on, let's dance.'

'I don't dance,' she protested but he took her by the arm and she let him lead her firmly to the dance floor, where an inch of space was left.

It was noisy and dim, full of elbows and heels and far, far too hot but, bizarrely, Kate enjoyed it. She hadn't danced since Matthew, but tonight that had no power to wound her.

Callan danced energetically, deliberately adding exaggerated movements to make her laugh. Kate felt herself relax into the evening. She was a good dancer, but it had been a long time since she had allowed herself to move in time to music, to give herself up to its rhythm and enjoy the moment.

It was a shock to glance at the clock over the bar and discover it was one in the morning. The party was thinning out now as people gathered coats and bags, called their thanks to Amy and headed either home or on to other parties. Kate and Callan were heading to the door of the club, too, when Callan realised he had forgotten his jacket.

'I'll catch up with you outside,' he

said apologetically.

Kate drifted with the crowd, listening to people chat and laugh. *I'm happy tonight*, she thought in wonder. It was an unusual feeling of buoyancy. She had left her worries aside for several delightful hours. Yes, they would return in the morning, but for now . . .

A man's strident voice broke into her thoughts. Then there was a peal of laughter that sounded familiar, and the man's harsh tones again. Kate was away from the brightly lit main street now, her heels clicking loudly on the pavement. Down a side lane crammed with parked cars she saw a glimpse of red dress. Melissa. Kate ran forward fearlessly.

It was dark in the lane. Melissa was swaying against a silver sports car, her arm held by a tall man who was speaking urgently to her. Melissa was answering him, her words slurred.

'What's going on?' Kate asked, stopping a little way down the lane. Was this Melissa's latest boyfriend? Was she about to make a fool of herself by interfering in a domestic tiff?

The man turned to face her, still holding Melissa's arm. 'It's none of your business,' he said, his eyes hostile.

'Do you know this man, Melissa?' Kate asked levelly.

Melissa shook her head slowly, but still with a dreamy smile on her face. 'He's offered me a lift home,' she said, her head falling forward, her face hidden by her tumbling curls.

The man let her go and she stumbled back against the car.

'Just go,' Kate said, making her voice as calm as possible.

He took a menacing step towards Kate but she stood her ground, thinking hard. She would not leave Melissa, that was a given, but what to do? Did she have time to reach into her bag for her mobile phone? Unlikely. Would he attack her? If he did, she would fight back — high heels could be a useful weapon.

'You interfering little . . . '

Kate bunched her fists, terrified but determined.

'The lady asked you to leave,' a deep, familiar Irish voice said behind them. It was Callan. Kate was flooded with relief. The man brushed past them silently and was gone.

Kate rushed to Melissa and supported her as her sister groaned.

'Oh Kate, my head hurts. I've drunk far too much. Please get me home.'

Together, Kate and Callan flagged down a taxi, shepherded Melissa into it and the three were carried home in the forgiving darkness and twinkling orange lights of the city to the Sheffield house.

Luckily the house was still and silent. Kate's mother had long gone to bed and Kate was able to get Melissa upstairs and tucked up with a large glass of water beside her in case she woke in the night.

Callan was waiting for her as she came back down to the living room. He had found the kettle and made two mugs of strong coffee.

'I'm sorry,' Kate said.

'Sorry for what? I had a lovely evening with you at the party. And afterwards, when you fought like a mother tiger for her cub to save your sister, I saw yet another admirable side to you, Kate — your loyalty to the people you love.'

'Melissa is a fantastic person. I wish you could have met her under different circumstances. We're none of us at our best lately, to be honest.' Then suddenly the words were spilling from her lips as she told him about their father passing away last winter and the ribbons that held the family together slowly slipping away.

'So Josh disappeared to busk in London and never gets in touch, Jenny isn't eating properly and is about to give up college and Melissa is partying too hard. Meanwhile Mum is lonely on her own and worries constantly about us all,' she finished up.

'And what about you, Kate?' Callan asked softly.

Kate looked surprised. 'I'm fine. I have to be. I've got to look after them. We are going to get through this. I'm going to get them through.' Her tone was determined, but it broke a little at the end and she covered it with a cough. 'So back to Invermalloch tomorrow. It's too late tonight now,' she said changing the subject as Callan reached for her. He sat back, his expression unreadable. 'There are fresh sheets and bed linen in the cupboard upstairs. You can have my old room. I'll sleep down here,' Kate chattered on, clearing away the mugs.

Callan's hands on her shoulders stilled her. He took the mugs from her hands and set them on the table, tilted her chin and kissed her briefly on her mouth. His lips were firm and warm, but before Kate could react, he was treading as lightly as a cat up the stairs and out of sight.

Kate's fingertips traced her own mouth in astonishment.

4

Mrs Bennett stood like a gaudy scarecrow at Kate's open back door. Her distinctive purple velvet hat was tipped rakishly onto her forehead but she had no free hand to push it back because she held a baby hedgehog in each. The colour in her full cheeks matched that of the rose patches on her long cotton skirt. Her knitted cardigan was caught with burrs from the plants in the lane hedgerows.

'Oh, goodness, pet, you gave me a shock, you did,' she said.

'Why is my back door open?' Kate replied distractedly.

She had arrived back at Invermalloch House after dropping Callan at his rented cottage in the village.

It had already been a strange morning, Kate mused, without finding her eccentric neighbour on the doorstep and her house unlocked and open. Callan had not attempted to kiss her again but was a relaxed and amusing companion as they made breakfast together for themselves, Kate's mother, Jenny and Melissa.

Kate decided she was glad he had not touched her or referred to the previous evening's kiss. Then she was annoyed that he seemed to have forgotten it or glossed over it. Finally she was swept along in his good humour and delighted that he managed to charm Jenny into eating a boiled egg and half a slice of toast. Melissa had managed a cup of weak tea before escaping back upstairs to bed, then Callan had helped Mrs Sheffield to wash up while Kate chatted to Jenny and tried to regain her trust.

She could hear her mother talking and Callan's answering murmurs and her chest was warm with . . . with *contentedness*, yes that was the word. For a little while all was well with the world. But the phone had rung then

45

and there was a rush to answer it in case it was Josh ... crestfallen faces — it was a sales call — and the world regained its fractured shape and Kate and Callan left soon after.

They drove home in companionable silence, broken only by comments on the weather and views as they headed north through the hills in their autumn glory to Invermalloch.

'It was open when I got here,' Mrs Bennett said. 'I came to bring you a pot of my famous green apple chutney and instead I found these two little chaps about to leave.'

Kate took Bob and Prickles gently from Mrs Bennett and went into the house. Her heart sank when she saw that the door to the living room was wide open. Carefully Kate put the hedgehogs into their box. Dreading what she would find, she went into the living room.

It was empty. Freddy and Loxy were gone. Kate's throat had a lump in it. She squeezed her eyes shut. They were ready to be released, of course they were, but she had planned it methodically. There was a safe glade far inside the woodlands, well away from people and roads and cars, where she had intended to free them.

Mrs Bennett's cheerful voice came behind her. 'You must have forgotten to lock up in your excitement at going to the party. Is anything missing?'

'Only my foxes.'

'Oh, dear, they'll be miles away by now I expect. Raiding someone's chicken coop, no doubt.'

Kate opened her mouth to explain that foxes mostly ate insects, worms and mice but shut it again wearily. *Please let them be okay*, she thought. Freddy and Loxy were still youngsters and like all young creatures, they were very curious. Without a mother to protect them, they would have no idea where curiosity finished and danger began. The woods were the only secure place. Kate hoped they would make their way there by instinct.

'How are you settling in?' Mrs Bennett asked from the comfort of the big sofa. 'I miss your gran. She and I were great chums, you know.'

'Gran relied on you a great deal,' Kate said. 'I know she enjoyed having you close by to pop in on.'

'And have you met your other neighbours, the Connaughies? What a lovely family. Young Davey's quite a charmer.'

'I haven't met them all,' admitted Kate. She hesitated, then met Mrs Bennett's bright blue eyes. 'Actually, I don't think Mrs Connaughie likes me very much at all.'

She fully expected Mrs Bennett to tell her not to be daft and that she was imagining it, but to her surprise Mrs Bennett threw back her head and gave a snort of laughter. 'Sally Connnaughie doesn't like any pretty, young woman within a mile of her husband! She was a Silly-Sally when she was a girl and she's a Silly-Sally now. I remember when we were just fifteen she had a nice

48

boyfriend called Paul, local boy. But she drove him away with her jealousy and possessiveness. She accused him of liking me better and the poor lad ran for the hills.'

Kate found it hard to imagine Mrs Bennett as a fifteen-year-old girl, but her story explained Mrs Connaughie's hostility towards Kate perfectly. Kate tried to recall what Mr Connaughie was like from the one time she had met him in the village. He had introduced himself politely as her neighbour and offered help if she ever needed fences mending or the like. Her impression was of a mild-mannered, kind older man of medium height and average features. It should have been laughable that Mrs Connaughie was so jealously protective of him but when Kate thought of the woman's sour face she didn't feel at all amused.

Mrs Bennett burrowed into one of her voluminous cardigan pockets, shedding burrs onto the carpet. She came up with a handful of post.

'These are yours, pet. The postie left them on the front step so I gathered them up for you.'

Kate took them reluctantly. A mustard coloured envelope was tucked in the middle of the bundle.

'Must get going. I'm off to collect all the rest of my windfall fruit today. Give my best to your gran when you see her.' Mrs Bennett sailed out of the house, knocking over a small vase of dried flowers with the swing of her full peasant skirt.

Kate righted the vase and took her time to re-arrange the honesty, lavender and poppy pods. Eventually, reluctantly, she tore open the mustard envelope. The message was stark: *IF YOU WON'T DO IT, I WILL. THE ANIMALS MUST GO.*

Kate dropped the note to the floor. First Gilly let loose to roam and getting sick. Then her house left open, the hedgehogs escaping and the foxes gone. Had she really left the house unlocked when she went to Glasgow? Or had someone found the spare key in the kitchen garden and then deliberately let the animals loose?

Kate shivered as goose-bumps rose along her arms. Someone maliciously wanted to wreck the rescue centre, wanted it gone.

It wasn't until later on that day that Kate realised there was no jar of chutney in the house. Yet wasn't that why Mrs Bennett had been there?

5

Oakview Terrace had not one oak in sight. It was ironically named, Kate always thought, for the poor oak trees had been chopped down to make way for the buildings. However, the blonde sandstone façade was pretty and the residents' apartments were light and airy, with high ceilings and solid walls. All in all, Gran had made a good choice for her retirement home.

'It was kind of you to give me a lift.' She turned to Callan who was reversing the car into a tiny space between a minibus and a people carrier.

'It's the least I could do since I failed so spectacularly to mend your car.' He smiled awkwardly.

Why, oh, why did his smile affect her so? That tug, that little pull she felt when she was with him. What was that? She gathered her bag and the chocolates for Gran, giving herself time for composure.

Kate's visit to her grandmother had almost come to a stop before it started when her car had begun to belch blue smoke that morning. Luckily Callan had dropped by to check on the foxes and had offered to lift the bonnet and investigate. She had hurriedly agreed, glad of a distraction so that she could think of a reason for the foxes being gone. She didn't want Callan or anyone else to know what had happened. She could deal with it; it wasn't anyone else's problem.

In spite of that, she was relieved when Callan offered to take her to Glasgow. On the bus, she would only be looking around at local people, wondering who hated her so much that they would break in to Invermalloch House and steal her animals away.

'Darling girl. You've come to visit — and brought a handsome young man, too. How delightful!'

Ailsa Sheffield clutched her zimmer

frame and manoevered, cautiously, towards them. She was tiny; a little sparrow of a woman with coiffured white hair and large grey eyes. As Kate embraced her tenderly, Callan knew who she reminded him of. In another sixty years' time, it could be Kate there. She was the image of her grandmother.

'Gran, this is Callan Jamieson. He's the new vet in Invermalloch while Morris is away.'

'A vet? Now that is useful. Perhaps you can have a look at Verdi for me. She's off her food and her fur is very dull.'

On cue, a large black cat eased its way out from under the sofa to stretch on the carpet at Ailsa Sheffield's feet. It turned its extraordinary jade eyes on her and blinked at her with feline love. Kate and Callan could hear its rough purr. Verdi did not seem to be suffering too much from lack of food.

'I'd be glad to,' Callan assured the old lady. He smiled inwardly. She not only looked like Kate, she acted like her too. How practical, on finding out his profession, to calmly ask him for his opinion on a pet. They had only just met, but he liked her immediately.

'Gran, I'm surprised you haven't tended Verdi yourself,' Kate teased.

'I'd love to. Blast these old bones of mine. They just will not do what they are asked to these days.'

Kate helped her to a seat while Callan spoke kindly to Verdi, stroking the cat and feeling its body for any wounds, broken bones or bruises.

Kate and Ailsa watched him.

'How is the rescue centre and my beloved house?'

There was no way Kate could tell her grandmother what had happened to Gilly and about the foxes and the threatening letters. She swallowed. 'The house is fine and the centre's busy. I've a herring gull just now and two baby hedgehogs. No doubt there will be more of those very soon with the cold weather coming on.'

'And I have no doubt you will do a

wonderful job of caring for them.' Ailsa Sheffield turned to Callan. 'Kate has a magical way with animals, you know. She can mend them most wonderfully. Even as a little girl she was a determined wee thing, savagely protective of her charges. Woe betide anyone who tried to persuade her to part with her creatures.'

'Poor Mum had a dreadful time trying to clean and tidy my bedroom,' laughed Kate. 'But it's thanks to you, Gran, that I had the skills.'

'And where did you get your skills to pass on, Mrs Sheffield?' asked Callan. He put Verdi down, rubbing the cat's ears and provoking another bout of purring.

'I was a nurse during the war. Well, it was a necessity in those days really. We all had to do our bit. I discovered I had a knack for making people feel better. They think it a modern research discovery that laughter and personal attention speed recovery, but we nurses knew it intuitively back then. What soldier wouldn't want a kind word and an extra biscuit slipped to them, when they had been through such terrible ordeals?

'After the war of course I didn't work, but I found I could use my skills on animals too. My sons weren't interested but when Kate was a child she was avid for knowledge about wildlife, so there we were. And here we are now — she's such a treasure. You look after her for me, young man.'

'I intend to,' Callan told her.

At the same time Kate was saying quickly, 'Oh, no, Gran, it's not like that. We're just friends.'

Ailsa looked at them shrewdly. Her grey eyes were startlingly clear for her age and unnervingly like Kate's, Callan thought. 'Well, well, let's share my chocolates, shall we?' the old lady said sweetly. She passed round the box. Kate concentrated on choosing between a cream caramel and a strawberry fondant. Sometimes her grandmother could be too perspicacious.

'Did you grow up in Ireland?' Ailsa asked Callan, once they had unwrapped the delicious treats.

'In part.' He paused. 'We were forever moving around. We must have travelled the length and breadth of the Emerald Isle. I was never in one school for more than a term or two.'

'Why was that?' Kate asked.

'My mother was something of a gypsy, you could say. There was a restlessness about her. She couldn't settle to anything for long. My brother and I would just be making friends at our new school, liking the house we were staying in and hoping we could stay this time. Then we'd come home to packed bags and we'd be off on the road again.'

'That's awful,' Kate said. 'How did you ever get enough education to become a vet? It must have been hard.'

Callan stroked Verdi, his gaze not on the cat but on his distant past. He looked darker than ever. Then he collected himself, picked the cat up and paced to the window.

'It wasn't all bad. I saw a lot of the country. I met a lot of interesting people. Somehow I always picked up quickly on the school work and by the time I had to study hard, I was living a more ordinary life with my mother's sister in Dublin.'

Kate hardly dared to ask more. But he suddenly beguiled her, this dark man who was so kind and gentle with animals and so polite and friendly to her mother and sisters and grandmother. No doubt his easiness with them was a result of having met so many people in a variety of different situations in his younger days.

'Where are they now? Your mother and brother?'

'My mother's dead. We were living in the north at the time. She left my brother and me at a shelter and went out to buy us a meal. She never came back. She was the victim of a hit and run driver, although no one was ever convicted for it. I don't suppose the death of a travelling person was too important in those days.'

'And your brother?' Kate whispered, horrified.

'Keiran chose a different path from mine. All I craved was normality. I wanted a clean home with food on the table and to know every minute of every day where I was going to be and what I was going to be doing. I was desperate for mundanity. But my brother had the gypsy blood. He took to the road shortly after we went to stay with my Auntie Siobhan and, like my mother, he never came back.'

Kate thought of Josh. What if he never came back? It was too awful to contemplate. Her heart went out to Callan.

She went to him and hugged him impulsively. His arms went round her and all at once she was no longer offering comfort but asking for more. Her skin was electric, each nerve aware of his warm skin and hard body.

She stepped back, confused. 'I'm so

sorry, Callan.' Sorry for what? For his terrible childhood or for her behaviour just there? Kate didn't know.

The zimmer creaked. Kate rushed to help her grandmother rise. The old lady touched her hair softly.

'Is that cat of mine all right, young man, or do I have to pay you some shocking amount of money for blasted pills?'

Kate was grateful. Her grandmother was helping her out, giving her time to calm herself. Callan played the game too.

He hadn't told anyone the story of his childhood until then. It had shaken him to tell it, but when the words started flowing he couldn't stop; he'd wanted to tell it, wanted Kate to hear it. Her calm grey eyes invited confidences and he had no regrets. She was trustworthy; unlike Annette, of that he was sure.

Kate's loving embrace had shaken him further for a very different reason. He had realised that he desired her with a passion that shocked him. He had stolen a light kiss on the evening of Amy's party but it had left him wanting more — much much more. But she was elusive and wary, like the wild animals she tended.

He hadn't expected her compassion for the telling of his tale, nor that it would turn into passion. He acknowledged the sensations, but did Kate?

'You can put your purse away safely,' he said to Ailsa Sheffield with warm humour. 'Verdi is as fit as a fiddle. She's probably had a cold or similar virus for a couple of days but I'm sure you'll find her appetite improving in the next day or so.'

6

The weeks were flying past. Suddenly it seemed all the shops had shed their Christmas goods and Easter eggs and toy chicks had already taken their place, despite the continuing cold weather.

The festive season had been a quiet one for the Sheffields and the gap left by Dad and Josh had been keenly felt. Callan had gone back to Ireland to see his aged aunt for a few days, and Kate had missed him.

The animal rescue centre was now very busy. It was the time of year when young hedgehogs were prone to wandering about instead of hibernating. Some youngsters were undersized and underweight, and it would be disastrous for them to hibernate without sufficient fat reserves to see them through the rest of the harsh winter months.

It was these little creatures that were

being brought to Kate by the villagers. She had sent round a home-made leaflet explaining the dangers to baby hedgehogs and people had responded kindly. It seemed as if the entire Invermalloch hedgehog population had ended up in Kate's kitchen!

She also had another bird — a large crow with a broken wing. The gull had been released and the crow, which was very talkative, had taken its place in the cage. Unusually, a grass snake had also been handed in. As far as Kate could see there was nothing wrong with it but the lady who had brought it had shuddered in disgust as she passed Kate the snake in a box. Her son had found it in the garden, and no, she did not want it back.

Grass snakes are not native to Scotland and Kate guessed it was a pet that had escaped. Callan had given it a clean bill of health and Kate had set up a clean vivarium tank with soil and moss and a large piece of bark for the snake to hide under.

Kate and Callan had met for coffee a couple of times to discuss patients but apart from that, Kate had seen no one and it had been far too hectic to phone or arrange time away.

Kate had just sunk down into her favourite, blue armchair when there was a knock at the kitchen door.

'Come in, it's open,' she called, too tired to get up. There wasn't even a fire lit in the fireplace, the cold ashes were a reminder of her waiting chores.

Callan was wearing a thick, cable-knit arran sweater and was a picture of bronzed vitality and good health. It was the complete opposite of how Kate felt; she was grey, drained and exhausted.

'Hello, Callan. Have you come to check up on your patients?'

'Actually, I've come to check up on you.'

He assessed her critically, his dark eyes crinkling, and shook his head solemnly. 'No, that cardigan is too thin. You'll need a thick sweater like mine, your winter jacket and boots. Oh, and a woolly hat.'

Kate was being chivvied upstairs to change. Bemused, she dressed warmly and returned to the kitchen to put on her leather ankle boots.

'That's better. Your carriage awaits, milady.'

In the car he solicitously tucked a blanket round her legs and handed her a flask. Kate opened the lid and smelt a waft of fragrant coffee.

'Mmm, delicious. Where are we going?'

'Wait and see. It's a magical, mystery tour.'

Kate saw she would get no more detail out of him and settled back to sip coffee and watch the landscape. The autumn leaves were long gone now, leaving dark-fingered trees stark against a tinfoil sky. She shivered.

'Cold?' Callan asked. He reached to turn up the car heater.

Kate shook her head. 'No, it's not that. It's silly really. I've discovered today that it's finally deeply winter. Christmas has been and gone so fast. We always got together at Mum and Dad's for Christmas, all of us; we never missed it. It was strange Josh and Dad not being there this year.'

Kate thought then of the delicious smell of her mother's tasty home-made mince pies which always greeted them as they returned to the family home from work, college, travelling or whatever they had been busy with. The house would smell warmly of spiced mincemeat and cloves and marzipan. A large Christmas cake always had pride of place on the dining room table and festive wreaths and tinsel were draped cheerily around the house.

Even as teenagers and young adults there was a scramble on Christmas morning to open stockings, followed by a breakfast of hot pancakes and maple syrup made by Kate and Melissa. They would then go for a walk while Mrs Sheffield prepared the lunch. Kate often chose to stay behind to help. It was a special time alone with her mother, thinking of the fun to come.

When the rest of the family returned, flushed and laughing from the cold, they would all sit together to enjoy the finest traditional meal of the year. The afternoon and evening were for relaxing and exchanging gifts.

'Dad would inevitably fall asleep on the sofa with his party hat still on,' she told Callan, laughing fondly at the memory. 'How he could nod off amid all the racket, I'll never know.'

Then she sighed. 'The next family celebration will be Gran's ninetieth birthday in March. We've always held the birthday parties at home too. It'll be very different this year. I don't know how we'll bear it.'

Callan put his hand reassuringly over hers and squeezed it gently.

'You are a strong, determined person, Kate, and you'll get through this. But remember, it's not a weakness to ask for help. We all need a little extra support at times like these.'

Kate held his hand for a moment before he returned it to the steering wheel. She looked out the window, the view blurry from her unshed tears.

They had reached the coast. It was a wild vista of tumbled rocks and pebble beaches with a pewter sea frilled with white foam. The gorse bushes on the edge of the single track road were stunted and shaped by the ever present wind. Even now at the end of the year, a few yellow blossoms clung to their spiky branches. Their rich egg yolk colour was strangely cheering amongst the shades of grey. They were like little pockets of hope, reminders of other seasons. Callan came round and opened Kate's door and a blast of chill air blew in.

'I found this wonderful place a few days ago when I needed some time alone. I immediately wanted to share it with you Kate.'

He led the way down a narrow shingle path that wound between gorse, willow and rowan until it opened out onto the deserted beach.

Callan found a spot sheltered by large boulders and put down the picnic hamper. He spread out two waterproof woollen picnic blankets and invited Kate to sit facing the sea.

'The show is about to begin,' he said mysteriously.

Kate munched on a thick ham sandwich and warmed her hands round a mug of lentil soup as she sat, sheltered from the wind by Callan, watching the sea swell and bubble.

'There,' Callan said softly. 'Isn't it nice to be taken care of sometimes?'

'I have to admit that it is,' Kate agreed, accepting another sandwich.

They grinned happily at each other. *I could get used to this*, Kate thought.

And what if you do and then he goes back to Ireland — what then? came a voice in her head. *Why take the risk? Better, surely, to stand on your own two feet and depend only upon yourself.*

Then, in the middle of all these

conflicting thoughts, Kate saw them. She sat perfectly still, aware of Callan beside her also intent on the sea. A pod of dolphins rose, breaking the surface gracefully, playing in the crests of the waves before disappearing for a minute or two. Again and again they returned, so close that Kate could see their big, intelligent eyes and friendly smiling snouts.

Kate leaned closer to Callan and reached for his hand. It was just as magical as he had promised. The two of them were alone on this majestic coastline watching a spectacular wildlife show that seemed as if it were put on specially for them. Just as quickly the dolphins vanished, presumably swimming deeper off shore hunting for food.

'Thank you,' Kate said simply. Impulsively she hugged Callan. He wrapped his arms around her tightly as though he never wanted to let go.

'Kate,' he murmured. Their lips were close but it was Kate who initiated the kiss. It was long, deep and passionate.

She was shaken by its intensity.

'I love you,' Callan said hoarsely; 'I can't help it, I've fallen in love with you, Kate Sheffield. Don't pull away. I know it's sudden but I'm prepared to wait and see if, in time, you might feel the same way about me.'

'I don't know what to say.' Kate plucked at the blanket. 'I like you very much.' She blushed, thinking of their kiss. Like, indeed! 'But I'm not the person you think you know. I don't know if I am capable any more of loving someone in that way.'

There was a silence between them. Kate glanced at him anxiously. Why did everything have to get so complicated?

Callan smiled and kissed her lightly on the tip of her nose. His dark eyes were tender as he rose to his feet. 'Come on, then — I'll race you to the spit. Last one there buys the drinks!'

With a joyful whoop, he was away. Kate leapt to her feet and ran after him, her feet crunching on the pebbles. The wind hit her face, her hair was dancing too and by the time she joined Callan on the narrow spit of land, she was puffed and tingling and exhilarated.

★ ★ ★

Later they found a charming, country pub in a little coastal village. The barman was a huge bear of a man who wore a kilt. A generous fire crackled in the hearth, over which hung claymores and shields.

'I'm nervous,' Callan whispered. 'Will they let an Irishman in, or will I have to battle it out?'

Kate nudged him and smiled politely at the man who had come to take their drinks orders.

They sat contentedly, Callan with a pint of ale and Kate with a tall glass of cranberry and lemonade.

'What you were saying about your Gran's birthday party,' Callan said. 'How about doing it completely differently? Have it at Invermalloch House instead. Start some new traditions;

change the menu. It might make it less painful for everyone and it would help your mum not to have to cook or clean in preparation of the day.'

'That's a brilliant idea. It might just work. I could clear the upstairs rooms for the family to stay in. The animals could be shifted to the box room for the day and Liss will help me cook, I'm sure.'

Then Kate rubbed her forehead. 'But Jenny isn't eating and Josh can't be found. Some family get-together, that will be.'

'Things may have changed by March. I was meaning to talk to you about Jenny. There's someone I want her to meet. As for Josh, he could walk across your doorstep tomorrow; don't give up hope.'

'What will you do in the spring break? Will you go home to Connemara?'

Callan shook his head and took a sip of his ale. 'No. I'd rather be here. And I don't intend to take more than a couple of days off.'

'Come to us for the party then,' Kate said impulsively.

'That is a very kind offer and I shall be happy to accept.'

Callan raised his glass to her. Kate raised hers too and they clinked glasses in an unspoken toast and a wish for a happy spring season to come with its promise of new beginnings.

★ ★ ★

It was late but Kate couldn't sleep. She sat clutching a mug of tea, with her legs up on the table in a way that would have made her mother tut reproachfully. Her head was swirling. Were she and Callan an item now? No, that was a terribly old-fashioned term. Boyfriend and girlfriend? They were a bit old for that. Partners? That sounded so cold and businesslike. Just good friends? But she didn't feel for any of her friends what she felt for Callan.

Kate wasn't even sure if she had friends any more anyway. She had let them all slide and fade away after Matthew had dumped her. Moyra, of course, was gone. But even Leila, Mary and Sue had given up and finally left her alone. Presumably they still met up for girls' nights out and days shopping, but they never called her and she didn't blame them. She had turned down all offers of help and companionship in her misery.

She had built a hard shell around herself and let no one inside. But the shell was cracking. Callan had broken through in a way no one else had been able to. Kate thought again of their shared kisses. He had kissed her thoroughly this evening before driving away from Invermalloch House. It felt wonderful, it felt right. He had told her he loved her. Could she ever feel the same way about him?

It was making her head ache. She sipped at the tea; it was tepid. It was as she got up to make a fresh cup, that Kate heard it. She froze. A knocking on glass. Then there was a screech and a groan. Kate relaxed again. The old hazel was moving its boughs on the games room window, that was all.

The rain that had threatened earlier in the day had arrived. Little glints of raindrops were visible against the velvet blackness in the outside light above the kitchen door. She left the teacup on the draining board and went through to the games room. It was full of shadowed, boxy shapes. Kate flipped the light switch. The shapes transformed into an ancient upright piano, a full size snooker table and everywhere cardboard boxes and tea chests were stacked in a higgledy-piggledy fashion.

The hazel tree was rubbing its scaly, lichened wood against the window; the sound was excruciating, like fingernails drawn along a blackboard.

'That's it. You're being pruned, here and now!'

Kate grabbed her waterproof jacket and ventured out the back door. Gilly butted her affectionately, the water dripping off her horns. Kate stroked

Gilly's soft nose and shone her torch into the kitchen garden. There was a shed in the corner that held the gardening tools. Kate fumbled inside for the pruning loppers. Gilly came into the shed, pushing Kate aside and bleating.

'Okay, you can stay here where it's dry. I'll leave the door ajar. Be good.'

The hem of her raincoat was acting as a drain, channelling rivulets of water onto her jeans which sucked them up greedily until the material was uncomfortably wet and heavy.

'I must be mad,' Kate told herself as tendrils of sodden hair stung her eyes and the wind whipped her hood away from her head. Brandishing the loppers she went through the rotting side door of the kitchen garden and round the side of the house, trudging across the long, rough grass to the games room window.

She stood on tiptoe to reach the offending branches. Before she could lop the uppermost limbs, there was a knock. Kate listened, puzzled. There it was again, a knocking. Coming from the front of the house. She gripped the loppers with ice-cold fingers. Was that the crunch of gravel? Was somebody there? Kate's chest was tight, her breathing raspy. If somebody was there at the front of the house, then only a few metres separated them from her.

Kate was suddenly acutely aware of the dark and the wind and the remorseless rain — and that Invermalloch House was very isolated. Her nearest neighbours were a good stretch away. Could she outrun whoever was there, to get help? Doubtful. Better to get back inside the house.

Slowly, carefully, she lowered the loppers and stepped away from the hazel. Then she was walking swiftly, then jogging and finally breaking into a run as if the devil himself was behind her snapping at her heels. She slammed the door and locked it. Her heart was hammering. She ran quickly to the front room and opened the curtains.

Beyond the rainswept grass were dark shadows — shrubs and hedges. It was easy to imagine a bulky human shape moving along the hedge line. Kate peered out, hands cupped to the glass but it was hard to tell. She was shaking with delayed reaction, shivering from being cold and wet. She shut the curtains and went to the hall. Without conscious thought her fingers dialled Callan's number.

'Hello?' His warm voice answered after a few rings.

'Callan!' She was flooded with relief. 'Callan, there was someone outside! I saw him, at least I think I did. He was knocking on the windows.'

'Kate, it's okay. Hold tight,' Callan said reassuringly. 'Lock the doors and windows. I'm coming round.'

Kate huddled in a blanket in her armchair until she heard the sound of a car coming up the lane. Then Callan was there at the back door. She could hear him talking to Gilly. She flung open the door and threw herself on him.

'Thank you for coming. I feel foolish for getting you out of bed for this.'

'I wasn't sleeping, just dozing on the couch. Good thing you phoned or my neck would have had an almighty crick in it by morning.'

Callan went round the house methodically, checking doors and windows were shut securely before he came back to the kitchen to find Kate. 'You're sure it wasn't some poor fellow come to your door to sell something or to ask for help?'

Kate's face fell. 'Oh no, I never thought of that!' Then she said thoughtfully, 'But whoever it was didn't ring the doorbell. I'm certain of that. I would have heard it anywhere in the house. No, it was someone creeping around, trying to scare me or ready to do some damage to the property.'

'What makes you say that?' Callan asked with surprise.

'Have a look at these,' Kate said simply. In her hand were three dark yellow envelopes.

Callan took them, mystified. He slid open the first one and pulled out a piece of paper that read, *GET THEE GONE. TAKE THE ANIMALS.* He looked at Kate. She gestured to the other two envelopes. He opened them carefully and read, *I WARNED YOU*, and finally, *IF YOU DON'T DO IT I WILL THE ANIMALS MUST GO.*

Callan sank back onto a kitchen chair and ran his fingers through his already tousled hair. 'Why, Kate? Why didn't you tell me this was going on?'

Kate shrugged. 'It was my business, I thought I could handle it by myself. I thought if I ignored the threats, they would get bored and stop.'

'But they haven't?' Callan guessed. 'What else? The goat's tether was cut, I saw that myself and wondered then what was going on.'

'I think someone poisoned Gilly. That same person came in to the house while I was in Glasgow and got rid of my fox cubs. I can only hope they let them go and didn't hurt them.'

Kate was crying now, not for her own terror this evening but imagining some faceless enemy being cruel to the animals at the rescue centre.

'We must call the police,' Callan said grimly.

'No!' she cried in panic.

He stared at her with dawning realisation. 'You know who is doing this, don't you?'

Kate shook her head. 'Not for certain, but I'm fairly sure.'

She paused, rubbed her eyes briskly and set her jaw in the determined way he had come to recognise. The barriers were back up. 'I was engaged to be married three years ago. To Matthew. He was my college sweetheart, what a cliché. But not only my sweetheart as it turned out — he jilted me two days before the wedding and took off with my best friend Moyra.'

'The cowardly so-and-so. My God, Kate, that's terrible! You think this Matthew is sending these letters? But why?'

'Actually I think it's Moyra,' Kate said slowly, 'She's been in contact with Mum a few times wanting to get back in touch with me. I wanted nothing to do with either of them. This is Moyra's way of retaliating.'

'It's possible, I suppose. But is there anyone else who might have a grudge against you?'

'I've been racking my brains to think if I have offended anyone. There's my neighbour, Mrs Connaughie. I don't know why but she doesn't like me.'

Callan studied the poison pen letters again.

'*Get thee gone . . .* ' he read out. 'That's quite dramatic, isn't it.' He spread them out on the table. 'Whoever it is doesn't like animals. Maybe the grudge isn't against you, but against the animal rescue centre.'

'In that case why didn't Gran get letters? I know she didn't, or she would have told the family. I think the person knows how much I love animals and that the easiest way to hurt me is by threatening them.'

'Can I borrow these?' Callan asked.

'Please take them. They make me feel sick. I just want them out of the house now,' she told him.

Then Callan was hugging her and caressing her and murmuring, 'That Matthew was a fool to give you up. But thank goodness for me that he did.'

And when they kissed, Kate forgot all about Matthew and the letters and gave herself up entirely to Callan's touch.

7

Callan opened his door the next day to a big surprise. 'Think of the devil and he shall appear,' he said.

'Isn't it 'speak of the devil'?' The woman turned to face him from the shelter of his own front door.

'Possibly, but I wasn't speaking of you, Annette, just thinking.'

Annette had always made him think of confectionery. Her hair was shiny, licorice swirls. Her skin was smooth caramel cream and her lipstick shade invariably candy pink. She looked good enough to eat. *But beware*, Callan reminded himself, she was more likely to devour him than the other way round. There was a pause while they assessed each other.

'Aren't you going to invite me in?' asked Annette.

At the same time, Callan said, 'What

brings you here?'

Annette's laugh tinkled prettily.

'Let me in and I'll explain. It's so cold! A hot chocolate would be lovely.'

So Callan found himself in his narrow, cramped cottage kitchen making hot chocolate for the very woman he had left Ireland to avoid.

'I checked on your house before I left,' Annette said, 'Everything is in order, but the place looks so empty and so soulless without you, Callan.'

He could quite easily imagine Annette poking around his property, peeking into the windows and trying the door handles. Anything to satiate her unending curiosity and her downright nosiness.

It was her obsession with him that had made him break off the relationship very soon after it had started. They had gone out together a handful of times and that was over a year ago, Callan realised. It had been a big mistake and one he regretted deeply. Once in his life and he on her radar, Annette could not be dislodged. Despite being just friends now, she could not leave him alone. In the end he had found it simpler to leave her and had left his home and his country to escape. He had hoped that a break would be enough to give her other occupations.

'Why are you here?' Callan asked bluntly.

Annette stopped her perusal of his bookcase, stroked her hand along the mantelpiece and turned back to him. 'I missed you. And to be honest I wasn't coping very well on my own. The boiler packing up at home was the last straw. I couldn't face it so I packed a bag and caught a flight over.'

Callan shook his head wearily. 'I can't always be there to fix and mend for you, Annette. It's time you took control of that.'

'I know I'm not your responsibility, Callan, I know that. I will get organised when I go back. But first I need a little holiday. And I thought of you.'

A chill went up his spine. Was he never to be rid of her? A suspicion grew and he asked, 'Where are you staying?'

Annette glanced around her and then appealingly back at him again.

'Could I stay with you? Just for a few days while I find a decent hotel.'

He almost fell for it. She looked so vulnerable. A few days wasn't a lot to ask, but she won't leave, he knew that. *She'll dig in and before you know it she will have made this cottage her home.*

'The Invermalloch Arms is very nice. I'll phone and book you a room,' Callan said firmly.

Annette lowered her lashes and her bottom lip trembled. She bit at it gently with perfect white teeth. Callan steeled himself. She would be fine at the Invermalloch Arms. He had stayed there himself when he first arrived. It was clean and adequate, if a little old-fashioned.

He made the call. As he escorted her down the street to the hotel he asked, 'What about your work while you're here? Did you mean what you said about being on holiday or will your work take up much of your time?'

Annette shrugged carelessly. 'I can work anywhere as long as my clients can contact me. I've got my smartphone and laptop so it's not a problem. Do you have a project for me?'

'No. It's not that, but I'll be busy myself with work so you'll need to occupy yourself most of the time.'

She certainly had enough luggage. It pulled at his arms as they walked along. It was ironic. He had thought to be free of her and yet here he was hefting her heavy bags while she tottered on her high heels carrying just a small leather Gucci purse.

Callan tried to visualise Kate behaving like that and failed. She was more likely to insist on carrying all her own luggage, even if it took her all day to reach the hotel. The strange thing was that he wanted to help Kate, yet he admired her independent spirit and lack of suffocating personality.

He left Annette and her many bags in the foyer of the Invermalloch Arms

Hotel and tried to ignore her sad little smile. No doubt he would see her again very soon. Invermalloch Village was small and Annette was desperate for his company.

As he strode back up to the cottage, Callan wondered whether Annette would settle to her work and leave him in peace after all, or whether she would constantly demand his attention. As he knew from personal experience, she could be extremely draining company.

* * *

Jenny was thinner; Kate could clearly see the shape of her skull under the tight skin of her face. Her hair looked lank and brittle even though it had been styled and pinned back cleverly. But she was in a buoyant mood and glad to see Kate and meet all the animals.

The crow had become very friendly and Jenny coaxed him onto her shoulder where he chattered non-stop and gently nibbled her earlobe.

91

'He'd make a super pet,' Jenny enthused. 'Wonder what Mum would say if I brought him home?'

'Especially if you then disappear to India for four months leaving her to look after him!' laughed Kate.

Jenny's face brightened. 'You are on my side, then! You think I should go to India with Heidi?'

Kate hugged her, feeling the delicate bones of Jenny's shoulders under her touch. It felt as if Kate could easily crunch those bones if she wanted to.

'I admit I got a shock when you announced your plan, Jenny. But you're twenty-one and old enough to decide for yourself. The only part I have reservations about is you giving up your college place. What about your future career?'

'You gave up your career to come here to Gran's and run the animal centre,' Jenny countered.

Kate sighed. 'That's different.'

Jenny scowled, immediately looking much younger and reminding Kate of their teenage years in the Sheffield home. 'There you go again, treating me like a child. It's one rule for you and another for me.'

'Don't fall out with me,' pleaded Kate. 'Callan will be here soon to take us out for the day. Let's put our differences aside and enjoy our time together. Please, Jenny?'

'Okay,' her younger sister agreed. 'We won't mention it. But it won't go away. It's my future, Kate, not yours.'

But not thinking and worrying about Jenny's future was harder for Kate to do. She was distracted by it as Callan drove them out of Invermalloch and south down the motorway. He and Jenny chatted easily, with Callan glancing from time to time at Kate to give reassurance. She was glad of his company. Even when they weren't talking they were communicating at some deeper level. She was very aware of his arm so close to hers and of the timbre of his rich voice. He smelled of soap and clean cotton shirt.

By the time they reached Ordmorn Farm she had put her worries about Jenny away to concentrate on enjoying the day ahead. She still hoped Jenny would come to her senses before she made a decision she might regret.

Callan drove expertly down a narrow road to a car park which was full of cars spilling out families and couples. It was a late winter Saturday and everywhere was busy with people keen to get out and about, but somewhere where there was warmth and shelter from the bitter cold.

'Chris Ord owns the farm,' Callan explained as they walked over to the farm buildings. There was a modern extension attached to the old stone house and through the glass Kate saw shelves of preserves, boxes of chocolates, cases of wine and displays of fine cheeses.

'Chris's dogs are patients of mine,' Callan went on. 'I've made a couple of home visits and it's such a wonderful place, I thought you two would like to come for a visit here.'

'It's not like any farm I've ever seen,' Jenny said as she browsed the packed shelves.

'As well as this shop, there's a café too with home baking. It's run as a farm by Chris, but the café and shop are extra businesses. I don't suppose farming alone is very lucrative these days.'

Callan waved as a tall, young man approached.

'Callan! Great to see you. Come on through to the office.'

Callan made the introductions. Kate was a great believer that handshakes were an indication of character. Chris Ord's handshake was firm and dry, a good sign. Out of the corner of her eye she watched Jenny straighten up and flick her fringe back. Clearly she was impressed by Chris too. Or did his thick, blond hair, piercing blue eyes and strong jaw have anything to do with it? Kate smiled. She was beginning to sense what Callan's plan was.

Chris led them through a door in the back of the shop. It led into a store room piled high with yet more jars and boxes of produce and goodies, and rows upon rows of eggs.

'Gosh, how many chickens do you need to produce that?' Jenny asked.

Kate hid another smile. It was the first time she had ever heard of an interest in farming from her little sister.

'We have three hundred chickens,' Chris told her. 'Nicky uses a lot of eggs for baking in the café. It's incredibly popular. I'll take you to meet her once we have finished here.'

Jenny seemed to shrink a little. Nicky must be Chris's wife or girlfriend. Silly of them to think a good-looking guy like Chris would be single. Callan winked at Kate. Whatever his plan was, he must think it was working. The office was in a room at the back of the store. Jenny gasped as she went in.

'Wow, you've got a Gary Fisher!' she exclaimed.

What on earth was she talking about?

Kate craned her neck to see Jenny and Chris looking at a bicycle which was hooked on the wall. It looked shiny, well-kept and sporty. Beyond that Kate had no idea as Chris and Jenny discussed technical details of the machine. She gathered it was an expensive, quality bicycle.

'Chris cycles a lot,' Callan said. 'Big trips around the Scottish islands and long distances abroad. Canada was the most recent, wasn't it, Chris?'

'That's right. Fill the panniers with gear, never forget the puncture kit and away I go,' Chris agreed cheerfully.

'I'm going cycling in India for four months,' Jenny told him excitedly.

A flash of surprise flitted across his face. He assessed her critically, taking in her gaunt frame. 'You know you need an awful lot of stamina to cycle day in, day out. Nicky puts me in training before a big trip. She was a dietician before she took on the café. That's why her cakes are organic, healthy and delicious. She designs a diet rich in carbs and protein to build me up before I go.' He paused and then said kindly, 'You look like a puff of wind would blow you away. Nicky could sort your diet, if you like? And you could cycle with us on weekends to get some training.'

Two collie dogs chose that moment to burst in, barking and wagging their tails furiously at the sight of Callan, and the moment was lost. Kate didn't know what Jenny would have answered. How keen was she to cycle in India? It was Heidi's idea, after all. Was it sufficient motivation for Jenny to start eating again? She was aware that Jenny seemed far more subdued as they watched Callan give the dogs a check-up and pronounce them fully recovered and fit for duty.

Chris took them over to the busy café, in another of the old stone buildings, one of the original parts of the farmstead. Inside, however, it was bright and modern with cream walls, glass-fronted cake cabinets and natural wooden tables and chairs. The walls were covered in paintings for sale and every table had a small vase of fresh flowers. The warm, sweet smell of baking pervaded the air and Kate felt her stomach rumble as a waitress went past carrying a tray of steaming soup bowls, crusty bread and shortcakes.

'Hi Callan, hi everyone.' A slender, blonde woman waved and came to greet them. She was at least ten years older than Chris with pixie-cut hair and subtle make-up accentuating her beautiful eyes and high cheekbones. She was elegantly dressed in a cream silk blouse and bootcut jeans and looked at ease with herself and the rest of the world.

'This is Nicky, my big sister,' Chris said warmly. 'I don't know what I would do without her.'

'You wouldn't cope at all,' teased Nicky fondly, reaching up to ruffle his hair as only older sisters can.

Chris introduced Kate and Jenny. Nicky shepherded them to a large, central table set for lunch. Jenny's mood had picked up as soon as the introductions were made and it was plain to Kate that her little sister was smitten with Chris Ord.

Lunch was delicious and Chris and Nicky were excellent company. Jenny managed some soup under Nicky's encouraging gaze.

It was as they were leaving, literally as Kate was lowering herself back into Callan's car, that Jenny spoke up. She looked shyly at Chris and Nicky. 'If the invitation still stands, I'd like to join you for a cycle, and . . . and I need help, please, Nicky with my diet. I've not been eating properly since my Dad died. Just not been hungry really . . . but I can see now that I need to change, to get fit and ready for India.'

Nicky hugged her impulsively and Chris grinned at her. 'Come up next weekend and we'll get started. Bring your cousin too, if you like, and we'll soon get you both in training.'

Jenny gazed at both of them with tears in her eyes. 'Thank you.'

It was heartfelt — and Kate realised that a corner had been turned. With luck, Jenny's journey back to health had begun. Her heart sang with relief.

Callan whistled all the way home. His idea had worked. He thought Chris and Jenny were well matched and Chris was a worthy motivation for Jenny to set out on her road to recovery.

8

The Spring Festival in Invermalloch was something quite special. For the rest of the year Invermalloch was a sleepy, tucked-away Highland village. In the summer there was a small influx of tourists to the few holiday cottages and converted crofts and a steady but moderate flow of day trippers to the two village cafes. But the Spring Festival was the highlight of the year. People came from all around the area and beyond especially for it.

Kate had been looking forward to it since Mrs Bennett had enthusiastically described it to her one day. She had been once before, years ago with her gran, and had a vague memory of colourful lights and sweet iced biscuits.

As she stepped into the village square now, Kate found herself smiling in delight. A massive welcome sign had been erected in the centre of the grass square. It sparkled cheerfully with a scattering of flickering chilli-shaped red electric lights and was topped by an enormous, ridiculous cut-out of a spring duckling. All around the edge of the square there were wooden stalls with candy-striped awnings.

Already the place was thronged with people buying trinkets, eating hot dogs slathered with mustard, and sipping from cups of mulled wine. The warm scent of sausages and pine smoke filled the air. It was like a scene from a Dickens novel, Kate thought; the only thing missing was a coating of snow! Spring was so late this year that it still felt more like winter.

Now all she had to do was find her family. She had arranged to meet them at the Festival and invited them to dinner at Invermalloch House. Callan had also promised to be there, although he had a few patients to attend to in the morning before he was free.

'Kate! Kate Sheffield! Hallooo.' A

great bellowing voice accosted her.

Kate looked over to the east side of the square to see Mrs Bennett waving frantically at her from behind a stall.

'Come along, dear! Support your local produce. Here, try some of this.' She handed Kate a plate and spoon. A small quantity of dark jam quivered on the plate. Mrs Bennett beamed, every inch the rosy-faced country woman selling her wares. Still like a Dickens novel! Kate grinned to herself.

The jam was delicious, sweet and tart and rich. Mrs Bennett's stall was piled high with jars of preserves — jams, chutneys and pickles glistening plumply under frilled caps and hand-scribbled labels. She was clearly doing well. Beside the jars was a wooden box full of money and a scrap of paper with sums totted up. Business was obviously brisk!

A small boy approached, pulling a tiny dachshund by its red lead.

'Oh, what a fine little fellow,' boomed Mrs Bennett.

Kate wasn't sure if she meant the boy

or the dog. The boy backed away, his money clutched tightly in his hand.

But Mrs Bennett had managed to squeeze out from behind her stall and enveloped the dog in a billow of discordant peasant cotton, Fair Isle sweater and silk scarves. 'What a sweetie. Do you know I have two just like this at home. I do love animals, don't you?'

The boy nodded cautiously.

Kate mumbled something about finding her mother and left them petting the dachshund who appeared to be quite enjoying all the attention.

Two stalls further down, there was a display of watercolour paintings. At first it was the frames which drew Kate's notice. They were unusual, being made of ceramic with dusty greys and smoky blue hues. She saw then that the paintings themselves were beautiful; local scenes from around Invermalloch which were finely detailed and rather lovely.

She looked up to see Mrs Connaughies's unfriendly gaze. Determined not to be put on the defensive, Kate gave her a deliberately light smile, fighting the urge to run.

'These are wonderful. I recognise Invermalloch Bay in this one. Whoever the artist is, they are really talented.' She was gabbling. *Stop it, calm down. I've down nothing wrong to this woman.*

Kate waited for a sour response from her hostile neighbour, but to her surprise Mrs Connaughie's face softened perceptibly and she looked proud as she told Kate, 'Thank you. I painted them. It's only a hobby but I always sell a few at this time of year.'

'I'd love to buy one,' Kate answered rather impulsively. 'How much is the one of the Bay?'

Just then Mr Connaughie and David arrived carrying boxes of eggs to sell. Mrs Connaughie straightened up with a quick flickering glance from her husband to Kate.

'That one's not for sale,' she said shortly.

'What a pity. I'll take the one of the hills instead, then.'

Mrs Connaughie wrapped it carefully in bubble-wrap. It seemed to Kate that she wasn't quite so severe as they exchanged money for the painting and she even managed to wish Kate an enjoyable day before barking at her husband who had dropped a box of eggs off the edge of a chair.

The crowd was thickening and Kate had to push her way through as carefully and politely as possible as she looked for the other Sheffields. She soon realised there were stalls and street performers in the side streets too and began to despair of ever meeting up with her family.

She had just caught sight of her mother when someone said, 'Kate?' and laid a hand on her shoulder to stop her.

She turned around to see Moyra. Instinctively she looked for Matthew too, but Moyra was alone. There was a long second when the two women simply assessed one another. Kate knew her own face was as stern as Mrs Connaughie's had been. In Moyra's, however she saw hesitation and a measure of supplication.

Moyra was not beautiful; she was not even attractive in an obvious way. She was stockily built with wide hips and thighs. A classic English pear shape, despite her Scottish ancestry. Her face was square and plain with a smattering of freckles across the bridge of her nose. Her brown hair was cut shoulder length with a blunt fringe that did nothing to enhance her looks. And yet she had ensnared Kate's Matthew, had made him fall in love with her, and in the end she had stolen him from her best friend.

'Moyra. I didn't expect to see you here,' Kate said lamely. She would rather not have to talk to Moyra but that was impossible given her proximity.

'I always come to the Spring Festival. It's a good place to pick up knick knacks for extra Easter gifts. Besides, Matthew's aunt lives in Wylie nearby as you probably know.'

She saw Kate glance about and said hastily, 'He's not here. He's got a nasty cold so decided to stay at home.'

There was an awkward silence between them, made more stark by the happy hustle and bustle of the crowd streaming around them.

'What do you want, Moyra?' Kate asked bluntly.

It was still painful to be near her ex-friend when memories of times together and a broken trust were still so raw.

Moyra's hands slipped protectively to her stomach as a man pushed past roughly. Kate's heart jolted; Moyra was pregnant. Her stockiness and a loose jersey had concealed it but there was no mistaking the bump outlined by her stroking fingers now.

'The baby is due in July,' Moyra said, 'We're so excited, so happy.' She paused, swallowed, and went on, 'I miss you Kate. Matthew does too, I know he does. We hurt you badly and I can't forgive myself, even now. We've tried to apologise but we can't make amends so easily. But . . . '

The fingers were busy again, moving gently, caressing and soothing and protecting Matthew's baby. 'There's a new life coming. We're going to be a real family and it's time to put the past to rest. You've always been a family person, Kate, so you'll understand what I am trying to say. It's time to move forward into a peaceful future. Please, please come and visit us.'

Before Kate could form a reply, Moyra had slipped a piece of card into her hand and vanished into a large marquee where music was playing with a slow and steady pulse.

Kate withdrew the card. Moyra had clearly planned on meeting her today. The card was pale violet with neat writing. Although it was script and not capitalised print, involuntarily Kate was comparing it with the poison pen letters. It was impossible to say whether they were written by the same person.

On the card Moyra had written a formal polite note inviting Kate to tea, giving directions to their house and a telephone number and email address to reply to. Kate read it again. She was ready to crumple and discard it but found herself hesitating. Slowly she folded it and slipped it into her pocket where she remained conscious of it all day long.

'There you are! Finally, dear. You need to go and see Melissa. She's making a fool of herself as usual.' Mrs Sheffield was flustered, her face flushed in spite of the chilly day, her breathing fast.

'Where's Betty?' Kate asked with concern.

'Oh, I know you said to bring her for company but I didn't want to bother her. Besides, she'll nag me to get out more and join her silly walking group.'

'Well she's right,' Kate retorted. She hugged her mother and guided her to a bench inside a heated tent where teas and coffees were being served. Mrs

Sheffield sighed with relief as she sat down and a girl came over with a tray of hot teas.

She sipped at the polystyrene cup, 'I miss you, Kate. What would I do if my heart went at home? How would I get help?'

'Jenny's there,' Kate reminded her mother gently.

'Jenny contributes to the state of my heart. She's still only nibbling at things like a church mouse. At least Chris is a distraction — and cycling is good for her, isn't it?'

'Yes, I'm sure it is but only if she's eating enough for energy. I thought, or I hoped, she had put all that behind her.' Kate sighed heavily.

Perhaps it was naïve to imagine that one visit to the Ords' farm could turn Jenny's life around. Her mother squeezed Kate's fingers anxiously.

'I'm sorry to burden you, love. It's not fair but I do rely on you. I feel so . . . so *shaky* lately. I can't seem to make decisions readily. Maybe it's old age.'

'You aren't that old, Mum. A lot has happened this year and you're still coming to terms with it, that's all. Once spring arrives properly with some warmth to it, I promise you'll feel so much better. Where are Liss and Jenny? I should go and get them.'

Her mother waved vaguely in the direction of the bandstand. 'Try to extricate Melissa from the mulled wine stand, will you. She was singing along very loudly with that young man and his guitar.'

Kate vowed to do her best and set off once more into the thick of it.

Before she reached the bandstand, she saw in the distance two figures walking down the hill from the cottages on the edge of Invermalloch. One was Callan. He was wandering along, hands in pockets, at ease with himself and the world. Kate had never known a man so comfortable in his own skin as Callan. He exuded an easy charm and confidence which usually calmed her own nerves. Her heart sang at the sight of him.

The other figure was a woman. She was chatting vivaciously, stumbling every so often on her wickedly high heels on the uneven cobbles. Whoever she was, they were clearly on familiar terms like old friends.

Kate waved. Callan caught sight of her and waved back. She waited for them to catch her up. The woman grabbed at Callan to prevent a fall and Kate noticed she did not immediately relinquish her grip on him, so that as all three met it was Kate who was the outsider, the gooseberry, to their couple. Her heart was no longer singing.

She fixed a polite smile. 'Hello, I'm Kate, and you must be . . . ?'

The other woman let a few heartbeats go by, just long enough to be rude. It was obvious that Callan had not told Kate anything about her. Then she gave a tinkling laugh and hugged close to Callan.

'Annette Tiverton. Surely Callan has

told you about me? I feel I know all about you, Kate.' She mock punched Callan's arm. 'It's very naughty of you, darling, not to tell Kate that I'm visiting with you.'

Alarm bells were sounding in Kate's ears but she nodded and smiled as if nothing was awry. Annette was beautiful. Her dark, glossy hair and creamy complexion were perfect. Her eyes were large and as dark in colour as Callan's. What a pair they made, Kate thought.

'Well you've met each other now,' Callan said mildly. He offered his other arm to Kate and guided them down to where the music was playing.

Melissa was there, dressed in a bright woollen, cerise shift dress and three-quarter length white leggings, with teetering heels to match Annette's. She was shiny with wine and the chill air and was singing lustily. On seeing them, she swooped down on Callan and insisted he dance with her. Other couples had started an impromptu ceilidh and there were whoops and hollers and peals of laughter as various people joined in the fun.

Kate had the momentary childish satisfaction of seeing Annette's expression of surprise as this unknown, attractive girl stole Callan away. She recovered herself quickly, though and was able to say to Kate in a cosy way, 'I love Callan's cottage, don't you? All the home comforts. I'm not missing my own place at all.'

It was Kate's turn to be surprised. 'You're living with Callan?'

Annette glanced from beneath lush black eyelashes. 'Didn't he tell you?'

They watched the ceilidh dancers, Annette following Callan and Melissa's progress through a very cramped version of A Dashing White Sergeant.

Was she being silly? It had been a few weeks since the trip to Ord Farm and she hadn't seen Callan in that time. They had both been hectic with work but had managed to phone to arrange today's outing. So why had he not mentioned Annette then?

* ★ ★

Dinner was a curiously lifeless affair, Callan thought. He was disappointed. He had been looking forward to seeing Kate's family again and between Kate, Melissa and Jenny he had expected a lively discussion with much banter and amusement. Instead Kate was withdrawn, her grey eyes neutral. She played the part of hostess perfectly but Callan, who felt he knew her well now, sensed a level of removal from him.

They had arrived in a lively enough manner back at Invermalloch House, with Melissa telling funny stories of her waitressing job in a loud, giggly voice. Her laugh was infectious and kept them all bubbling as they strode along the sparsely vegetated lanes and watched the redwings flying along the hedge lines. Kate had seemed happy enough, smiling in the right places at the anecdotes and helping her mother along with the crook of an arm.

He had wanted right then and there

to give her a crushing hug and kisses. She looked in her natural setting, at the centre of her family, caring for them. He caught her eye and winked. She half-smiled but at that moment Annette, who had been invited by Kate to join them for dinner, had chosen to bend her head to his to whisper about her blisters. Kate turned back to her mother and the moment was lost.

Annette was putting herself out to be a pleasant companion. She had stayed meekly in the hotel for a week before asking him nicely if she could stay with him for a little while as the hotel had a problem with the plumbing and her ensuite had no hot water. Callan could hardly refuse. But she had not intruded on his work or his time and he began to think that her need for him was gone. She was now simply a good friend and he was relieved. Soon she would return to Ireland, out of his way.

The big dining table at Invermalloch House had been cleared of junk and replaced with settings for a meal. Kate added another setting for Annette and served up steaming hot lentil soup and crusty bread.

'Do you have to keep that thing there?' Annette shuddered dramatically, pointing one of her beautifully mani-cured vermilion-nailed fingers at the antique sideboard.

Kate glanced over to where a large glass vivarium sat centre place on the sideboard top. It was hard to see what was in it at first, other than soil and moss and a large granite stone. Then the snake slid sinuously along the panel showing its magnificent yellow belly scales, all rippling muscle. Annette squirmed in her seat and put her spoon down deliberately.

The crow chose that moment to caw loudly from the games room and they could all hear the splatter of something unmentionable hitting wood.

Kate shut the door in the hope that the crow would quieten. He was very smart and liked lots of attention, and new people were of particular interest.

Somehow Kate didn't think Annette would enjoy having a large bird perched on her shoulder nibbling her earlobes.

'Sorry, I can't move the vivarium, it's too heavy, but I'll drape it. I know some people have a thing about snakes,' she said to Annette.

'I don't have a 'thing' about them as you call it,' Annette retorted indignantly. 'I simply think it's disgusting to eat where animals are around.'

She looked around her in distaste. The room was shabby, the bookshelves lopsided from crammed books, the curtains decidedly dusty from neglect and the air probably full of animal germs. There was a musty smell emanating from the direction of the vivarium.

'Sammy does smell a bit musky,' Kate admitted, guessing Annette's thoughts from her wrinkled nose and pained expression, 'Unfortunately grass snakes do smell a little.'

'Never mind, dear,' Mrs Sheffield soothed Annette, adding helpfully,

'Your soup's getting cold. Better eat up.'

Annette went white. Kate assumed it was with rage. Callan, who had been eating quietly, thought she looked ill.

He touched her shoulder with concern. 'Are you okay? Look, I'll help Kate move the snake. Kate's right, lots of people don't like them. It's nothing to be embarrassed about.'

'I'm not embarrassed,' hissed Annette furiously. 'Don't bother moving the horrid creature on my account. But I really do think . . . '

They never found out what she really did think because at that moment her phone rang and she excused herself to take the call in the hallway.

Kate was fuming now, too. She had invited Annette to lunch because she was Callan's friend. Did the woman have to insult her and her home? And did Callan have to stick up for Annette quite so readily?

'I have to go. That was a business call,' Annette put her head round the door, not coming all the way in, 'It's my best client so do please excuse me. I'll make my own way out.'

Kate politely rose to see her to the door anyway. Her flare of anger had died fast and she felt guilty. Perhaps Annette really did have a snake phobia. And, Kate admitted to herself, she did have an unusual job and a run-down house. Gran hadn't maintained Invermalloch House in recent years due to her infirmity and Kate had no time or spare cash to do so. She could imagine Annette's home as tidy and modern, and most definitely pet-free.

'I'll get your coat,' Callan said. 'It's a shame you have to leave so early but perhaps we can all meet up again another time at my cottage?'

Mrs Sheffield, Melissa and Jenny all nodded, smiling.

'What a lovely idea,' breathed Annette smiling back sweetly. She turned deliberately to Callan as he went to join her at the door. 'Oh, and darling, don't worry about dinner, I'll cook tonight.'

They went out, Kate unable to see Callan's expression at Annette's final remark. Why did she get the feeling it was aimed at her instead of him?

'They seem really close,' Melissa remarked. 'You'd better stake your claim Kate. Annette's smitten with him, that's obvious.'

'Callan prefers Kate — how could he not?' chipped in Jenny loyally.

'I don't want you getting hurt,' Mrs Sheffield said, 'Just be careful, love. Is he worth it?'

Kate put her bread back on her plate. She couldn't swallow it for the constriction in her throat. 'Stop it, all of you,' she said quietly. 'Please. I don't want to discuss it. I'm going to go and do the washing-up. And no, I don't want any help, Melissa. Stay here and enjoy the food.'

She folded her napkin methodically and put it on the dining table. Then she went into the kitchen and filled up the big basin with hot water and suds.

Moments later Callan joined her. He went to hug her. She moved away.

'What's the matter, Kate?'

She crashed a dish in the sink. 'Nothing's the matter. Why should it be?'

'You tell me. You hardly look at me, you don't want me to touch you. Something's bothering you.'

She thrust him a plate to dry. 'Why didn't you tell me about Annette?'

'There's nothing to tell. She's an old friend. She needed a place to stay. Wait . . . you're not jealous of Annette, are you?'

'Of course not.' She looked ferociously at the frothy water in the sink as she scrubbed the oven dish hard.

'This is very unlike you, Kate. I'm surprised,' Callan remarked. 'One of the things I like best about you is that you don't get flustered.'

'So you don't like me now?'

'Don't be absurd! You should know by now that I love you — even when you annoy me.' Callan kept his tone deliberately light.

'So I annoy you, do I? Well, don't worry, I'm sure you will find Annette a perfect antidote to me. She looks more than capable of pleasing you so why don't you hurry on home to her?' Kate slammed the rest of the crockery into the sink and heard it crack horribly.

'Don't be silly. You're overreacting. Calm down.'

Kate was all of a sudden icily calm. Her rage was gone, replaced with an emotion so hurtful she did not want to identify it.

'You know,' she said carefully, meeting Callan's eyes for the first time, 'Those are the exact same words Matthew said to me when I challenged him about Moyra.'

'You're being ridiculous!' Callan's temper, always slow to rise, began to burn hard. His tone was sharp, the Irish tones accentuated by anger.

'Please, just leave now,' Kate said

quietly. 'I need some time to think.'

'You're being a fool, Kate Sheffield. I'll leave now, but I'll be back.'

Callan flung the teatowel onto the table and closed the door loudly behind him. The room resonated.

Kate heard a murmur of voices, the sound of sharp footsteps in the hall and then the front door being opened and shut with no great care. The house was silent. Callan had gone.

Her eyes were dry. Mechanically she took the broken pieces of china out of the sink and dropped them in the bin. She watched numbly as beads of crimson blood welled on her fingertip. The ceramic plate edge was razor sharp. There was no pain for a moment. Then the cut began to sting.

Suddenly Kate was sobbing wildly. She ran upstairs and curled on the bed, hugging her knees to her chest to keep out the world. She barely heard her mother climbing the stairs and Melissa calling her back down.

She fell asleep exhausted, and woke

later that evening to an empty house. She felt hollow and empty.

What had she done? What had Callan done?

9

It snowed in the night. Kate awoke to the muffled silence that only a heavy blanket of snow produces. The singular sound was the sharp, clear clip clopping of hooves on the kitchen tiled floor. Gilly had yet again managed to butt open the back door and was now on the prowl in the kitchen, nibbling at the blue comforter in the old armchair and flicking her stumpy tail happily.

Kate pulled back the bedroom curtains and stared out. It was half light; that dull spring darkness that is slow to shift in the mornings. The ground was paler than the navy sky with hummocks, fences and hedge lines softened and rounded by the deep snowfall into an unknown landscape.

For a moment Kate soaked up the view, taking pleasure in the glint of the tardy moon on the crystal surface. Then she remembered and her mood plummeted. Callan was gone. She went downstairs.

Gilly greeted her with a friendly snort through flared nostrils.

'Come on girl. I know it's cold out there but you can shelter in the shed.'

Kate shivered involuntarily; it really was freezing. Only two weeks to go until Gran's ninetieth birthday party — March was well on its way now and yet it was as if the world was determined to hang on to the winter darkness.

She wrapped her dressing gown tightly round her and pulled Gilly out into the kitchen garden. The big birthday celebration was looming and she was completely unprepared. It had crept up suddenly and she had been so preoccupied with her family's problems and then her own that she had done no shopping or cleaning or any kind of preparation in the house.

The only thing she had achieved was to invite everyone to Invermalloch

House for the day. She could still hear her mother's tone of surprise as she agreed. Melissa and Jenny were both pleased at the idea. It would be the first time they had held Gran's birthday party away from the Sheffield home. But Callan was right. It would be less painful this way.

Callan. His name popped into her thoughts every few minutes. He had become such a solid part of her life so quickly. And she had sent him away. Matthew's words coming from Callan's mouth had twisted her insides cruelly and destroyed her trust of him. Made her want to scream and shout and cry with loneliness and betrayal. And yet, what had he said?

Slowly his words came back to her. Callan Jamieson was in love with her! But she had forced him to go. Kate's cheeks burned as she remembered how she had accused him of cheating on her and of loving Annette instead.

She ran upstairs again in agitation. Maybe she could catch him and explain. She would apologise and ask him to let them start afresh.

She loved him. It was simple. Kate threw on a pair of faded blue jeans, thick knitted sweater and her coat, kicked her feet into her knee-length leather boots and clattered down to the car. She brushed several inches of soft, grainy snow from the windscreen and backed the car carefully down the white lane. She knew where Callan's cottage was. It was one of a set of twin houses at the top of the village. With any luck he was still there, holed up against the harsh weather and brooding on her.

Kate was focused so entirely on Callan and what she would say to him that she received a very real shock when Annette answered her ring at the door. All at once her insecurities came flooding back. Perhaps he really had chosen this beautiful sultry woman above plain Kate Sheffield.

'Kate. How lovely,' Annette purred. 'I was hoping to see you today. Come in, please.'

She didn't look to see if Kate was following her but led the way confidently through the tiny, narrow hall as if she owned the place. She gestured to Kate to take a seat in the prettiest sitting room Kate had ever seen. It had low, round stone-edged windows beyond which a small snow-laden lawn could be glimpsed. The stone window-sills held displays of glasswork and pottery all in different shades of blues and greens giving a soothing underwater effect.

The room was furnished in warm walnut chairs, bookcases and a grandmother clock. Colourful cushions and throws gave the room a relaxed and welcoming feel. Kate could imagine Callan in here reading or writing up his day's reports from the surgery.

'He's not here, you know,' Annette said softly.

Kate sank down into a scatter of aquamarine and dark blue silk pillows. It was so soft she felt she could stay there forever, hiding from her misery.

'Where's he gone?' she whispered. A strand of hair crossed her forehead and she pushed it behind her ear with a nervous flick.

'Back to Ireland,' Annette told her, dark eyes widely innocent as she looked at Kate.

'He has a beautiful house in Connemara. I'm very fond of it myself,' she sighed sweetly as if reliving wonderful memories, 'Good times indeed.'

There was a silence between them. Kate heard the rough caw of a crow as it landed heavily on a snowy bough outside. There was the roar of a four by four going far too fast down the village High Street.

Callan wasn't even on the same island as her any more. He was away across a sea that was distant, both physically and emotionally. Annette sat beside her and took her hand. Her skin was warm and faintly damp.

'Don't blame yourself Kate. It's Callan. He's like that. Whenever things become intense he just takes off.'

Kate shifted slightly and removed her hand from Annette's grasp.

Annette smiled again sympathetically. 'Yes, he and I have a very intense relationship you know. He loves me passionately and wants us to get married. But then he took off over here for some space. I wasn't worried. I knew he would return to me and to Connemara. Sometimes Callan needs breathing space from all that love.'

She smoothed her skirt across her legs and slid a glance at Kate.

'As I say, Kate, don't blame yourself. It wasn't you that sent Callan fleeing. It was me. He's waiting for me in Connemara right now. I'll give it a week or two, then follow him back.'

Kate's thoughts were in turmoil. She didn't now know what to believe. Was it true? It made sense the way Annette told it. But it meant that Callan had lied to Kate when he told her that he loved her during their terrible argument. She struggled free of the cloying cushions and made to rise.

Annette said suddenly, 'Don't go. There was something Callan wanted me to give back to you.'

She moved across to the walnut dresser and slide open a drawer.

Kate waited. What had Callan left for her? A letter, explaining why he was leaving her? Describing his obsession with Annette and his need for her and for the stunning wilds of the west coast of Eire? She rubbed her forehead tiredly. Then she glanced up at Annette and froze. Annette held three mustard envelopes, fanned like a sick hand of cards.

'Callan gave you my letters?' It seemed impossible that he should have given Kate's most personal, most vulnerable secrets to this woman. A woman who, Kate was sure, disliked her almost as much as Kate did her.

Annette shrugged. She picked up a slim black laptop and a file of papers and set them on the coffee table between them. She was preparing to work, her body language said, and was no longer interested in Kate.

'Callan told me he was concerned about you,' she admitted casually, 'He told me about your anonymous correspondent.'

Kate could imagine Annette wheedling it out of Callan who was too honest and straightforward to dissemble. He would have told her in the end.

Annette opened up the laptop as if Kate was no longer there in the room with her, and clicked on the keyboard with one hand, while scribbling on a piece of yellow paper with the other.

And that did it. Little bits of memory slid into place for Kate. The horror of the dark yellow envelopes on the floor at Invermalloch, these same envelopes fanned in Annette's hand and a similar — no, identical — envelope being used as a convenient notepad to calculate sums of money made at the spring festival. The envelopes were an unusual colour. How likely was it that another person was sending them? How careless of Mrs Bennett to use one in plain view of Kate that day. A tiny slip, but one that had most definitely given her away. Kate could hardly believe it.

Not Moyra, then — the invitation to tea was genuine after all. Not Mrs Connaughie, who gave every appearance of being the traditional country housewife. The author of the poison pen letters had to be Mrs Bennett.

Mrs Bennett, who was Kate's Gran's best friend and Kate's good neighbour. Kate thought back to the day she had arrived home to find the back door open and her foxes gone. She had caught Mrs Bennett red-handed and not realised it. Mrs Bennett had even had the cheek to hand Kate a letter directly, claiming the postman had left it!

Everything was collapsing around her. She had lost Callan, whether to Annette, to Ireland or something else she didn't know. She had lost her dear father. Her family were drowning in grief. Moyra was pregnant by a man that Kate could still not completely forget and now the animal rescue centre, which had been her refuge, her sanctuary, was revealed as threatened by a woman she had considered a friend and ally. She was no friend, instead she was bent on destroying the one security that Kate had. It was too much.

Annette was looking at her curiously, eyes narrowed, assessing Kate's reaction. 'Clearly you know who is responsible,' she breathed. 'Do tell.'

'I have to go,' Kate said abruptly.

She hurried from the cottage, fumbling with her car keys. She sat in the front seat of the car, shivering. A pale watery sun was up but there was no sign of a thaw. Dark clouds on the horizon suggested that another fall of snow was on its way.

But the icy coldness lay within Kate. She hugged her coat to her tightly and felt something crinkle in its pocket. Her searching fingers found the folded lilac paper. Slowly Kate opened it and re-read Moyra and Matthew's invitation. Kate was steady and tenacious by nature. She was not going to crumble. Everything was a mess it was true but she had to put it right.

She would challenge Mrs Bennett about the letters, soon, and find out why she had done it. But first Kate had a call to make.

Her icy fingers tapped the numbers on her mobile phone. There was a ringing tone then someone picked up. Kate took a deep breath.

'Hello, Moyra.'

10

'Hello dear. Come along inside.' Mrs Bennett seemed pleased and surprised to see her. Kate followed her along the dark hallway into the living room. She noticed for the first time that Mrs Bennett had a slight limp as she walked. It lifted her wide hips to a higgled movement as she shuffled in fluffy house slippers across the parquet floor.

The house was architecturally the same as Invermalloch House but where Kate had made the kitchen the centre of the house, here the back room, which served as a games room at Invermalloch, was clearly the place that Mrs Bennett spent most of her time in. Like the rest of the house it was all dark panelled wood and thick old flowered carpets. It also smelt pungently of tomato soup and dogs.

One side of the room was taken up

with an enormous mahogany bookcase. Instead of the rows of books Kate had at Invermalloch, it was full of dolls. The dolls were encased, each in a glass or plastic cylinder and each wore the national dress of a multitude of nations. Kate remembered how, years before, an aunt had brought her back such a doll from Canada. It was dressed in red and white with maple leaf patterns. Kate, the child, had immediately freed her dolly from its showcase to play with it.

Goodness knows where it was now. Probably hairless and grubby, gracing a landfill tip somewhere. But these dolls were pristine. Their eyes seemed to follow Kate from their glass prisons as she moved to take a chair.

Two fat dachshunds yipped and waddled over to greet her.

'Down Mitzi, down Lilly!' barked Mrs Bennett, giving each little dog an affectionate tap on its head. 'Naughty girls. Find your baskets. Go on.'

They ignored her and fixed their liquid eyes on Kate hoping for a treat. A waft of doggy smell exuded from them. Kate turned away with a cough.

On the other side of the room were two shelves crammed with framed photographs. Most were faded black and white images. There was one of the late Mr Bennett as a handsome young man dressed in Royal Air Force uniform from his time in the Second World War. There were Mr and Mrs Bennett on their wedding day. Even in black and white Kate could see Mrs Bennett's rosy cheeks. She looked glowing and happy in her pearls and white gown with long gloves and fifties style shoes.

There were other family groupings, with people wearing wide lapels and bell-bottomed trousers. The colour of the photos was faded and yellow-tinged. There were a very few modern shots of one child showing a progression from soft, fat baby to chubby toddler to a gap-grinned boy with tousled hair.

Kate searched the images until she found it. At the back on the top shelf there was a picture of Mrs Bennett and Kate's Gran laughing to the camera, sharing a joke with the unknown photographer. It took the breath from Kate. It was why she was here. She frowned and turned back to the old woman who had started to ask whether she would take tea.

She faltered at Kate's look. Put one hand to her throat, used the other to find her way to an armchair. 'You know,' she whispered. It was a statement not a question. Her ruddy cheeks had blanched. She looked ill.

'Why?' Kate asked simply.

Mrs Bennett's big face crumpled. 'I'm sorry, I'm so very sorry. I don't know why. It was an awful thing to do.'

'Have you any idea of how terrifying it was?' Kate asked more sharply. 'Waiting for the postman, dreading his arrival, wondering what vindictive mail he was going to bring? I felt sick each time.'

She paused and swallowed. 'And then to find out it was *you*. My

143

neighbour. Someone I thought was my friend. Someone I could rely on, or so I imagined. It beggars belief.'

Mrs Bennett mopped her eyes with a large red handkerchief. Her hands were shaking. Kate almost felt sorry for her.

'You let Gilly loose, you made her ill by feeding her something bad. You released my foxes before they were ready. And my baby hedgehogs were about to go the same way, weren't they? If I hadn't arrived home just then, you'd have dumped them. I think it was you scaring me that night scratching at the window too. Why do you hate me so much?'

'No, no,' Mrs Bennett howled. 'It's not like that my dear. I don't hate you. Of course not. It was the animals. I wanted rid of them.'

'But you love animals!' Kate said, bewildered, gesturing to the two dogs curled now together into a wicker basket.

'I love *pet* animals. But that's different from some of the vermin up there. Dirty things!' This was said with a dramatic shudder.

Kate waited. She was suddenly sure there was more to this story than she had first thought. Sure enough, Mrs Bennett at once gave a huge sigh and began to speak again as if by confessing, she could lighten her burden.

'It all started while your gran was living at Invermalloch House. As you know we'd been neighbours and friends for many years. Your gran was always so good to me.'

Mrs Bennett fetched the picture in its frame and looked at it fondly, remembering good and better times perhaps.

'Then a couple of years ago, she took this foolish notion of running an animal rescue centre. I tried to talk her out of it but she was adamant.'

'My grandad died,' Kate said. 'She needed to fill the gap, be useful.'

Mrs Bennett nodded in agreement. 'At the same time my son was trying to persuade me to sell up and buy a place in Devon nearer to him and his wife.

My hip was getting worse and I also wanted more time with Nicholas, my grandson. So I agreed when he told me he had found a buyer. Unfortunately the day the buyer came, your grandmother's goat escaped and ate all the flowers and kicked up my lawn. It was a terrible mess. There was no sale that day.'

Kate got up and brought Mrs Bennett a glass of water. She sipped gratefully and continued.

'There were other interested parties as it turned out. But the rescued foxes, once released, stayed close because they were tame and there was food for them. They terrorised my little dogs, broke up the lawn with their digging and left their droppings everywhere. No one would buy. I thought when your Gran went into the nursing home the rescue centre would fold and I could sell my house.'

'And then I appeared,' Kate said slowly.

Mrs Bennett blew her nose loudly

into the red handkerchief. Her colour was better and she looked relieved that she had finally told her story.

'You appeared,' she agreed. 'I couldn't tell you any of this. You'd lost your father, your gran was ill and you were clearly keen to keep on with the centre. It was cowardly I know, but I had to get you to give it up voluntarily, so I came up with the letters. I never imagined it would cause you so much fear. I suppose I thought you would see sense and think it not worth the effort to keep it going. And I never, never poisoned your goat, I wouldn't be cruel to animals. As to scaring you, not in a million years. Perhaps it was a branch scratching your window but not me. Heavens, pet, I can hardly walk to the village these days with my hip.'

There was silence in the room. It was only letters, then. Cowardly, yes, but dangerous no. Gilly had eaten a plant that had disagreed with her but thankfully it was not a malicious act. The intruder at the window was most likely a branch whipped up by the wind or possibly a bird pecking on the glass. She would never know — but her heart lightened to know there had been no human threat.

Kate watched the motes of dust swirling in a shaft of spring sunlight in the dark, old room. Mrs Bennett still had a few bedraggled Christmas decorations in her house. Was she, like Kate, too disorganised and worried about other things to tidy up and welcome in the fresh new year, or had she hoped in her heart to have sold up by now and to be playing with her grandson in a neat, modern bungalow in Devon?

'What are you doing for the spring break, Mrs Bennett?'

The older woman was startled by the abrupt change of subject.

'Staying here. It's too far with my hip to go to my son's although they have offered. His wife's a dear girl, and Nicholas is a charming little chap. The pain is worse if I sit too long so I don't fancy flying or indeed going by train for hours and hours.'

'Will you come to Invermalloch House then to help celebrate Gran's birthday in March?' Kate asked.

Mrs Bennett's eyes welled up again.

'Would you want me, dear, after what I've done?'

'It was a tale with two sides, as are all tales. I very much want you to come to Invermalloch, and Gran will be delighted to see you.'

She left Mrs Bennett comfortable with a pot of fresh tea, sitting next to her beloved pet companions, and wandered slowly home down the lane cloaked in its hedges, listening to the steady drip of melting snow.

Hints of spring were appearing after the rapid thaw, giving hope — scattered clumps of snowdrops bravely flowering with their delicate green tracing on the petals and the vividness of their leaves. There was even a frog moving slowly along the hedge bank, one of the first to emerge, beautifully patterned in gold and peat-brown.

Kate fed Gilly the goat and made sure her tether was secure. The crow welcomed her with raucous coughs. The hedgehogs rustled sleepily in their box houses. She lit a fire, starting with newspaper and wood kindling then as the flames licked more confidently building up with coal until she had an intense red glow of heat and the kitchen was cosy.

Kate sat in the blue armchair and saw patterns in the flames, faces in the burning coals and snakes in the smoky ropes going up the blackened chimney. She was sure of two things now. Callan would return. Annette's conversations about Connemara and their relationship were all smoke and mirrors. Callan had said he was in love with Kate and that he would be back.

Mrs Bennett's story had shown her that many things lay behind what at first seemed simple. But things were never as they first appeared. So Kate clung firmly to Callan's words and trusted finally that they were true.

Secondly, the animal rescue centre had to go. And Kate, too, would leave as soon as Gran's birthday was over. It had been her refuge for a while but it was time to move on. She would find homes for the animals, then help Mrs Bennett prepare for selling her house.

Kate stoked up the fire and watched the smoke rise.

11

Moyra and Matthew lived in a tiny box bungalow in a new estate at the edge of the town of Cromarth. Kate drove cautiously along the narrow avenue which was barricaded on both sides by parked cars, until she found number fifteen Willow Avenue.

Every house was identical in shape and size but all were neatly tended and still had that freshly moved-in feel of a just-completed estate. People had made efforts to individualise their properties by hanging name-plates, painting front doors different colours and by creating flower beds and planting pampas grasses in the pocket front lawns.

Number fifteen had a maroon main door, and Kate remembered that this was Moyra's favourite colour. A flower-bed had been dug out all around the lawn. The soil was dark and rich and solid with frost, but a few hardy crocus leaves had broken through. A spade still stood upright like a sentry in the earth. There were no other plants and Kate guessed it was a project which had been abandoned due to Moyra's pregnancy.

She rang the bell and waited. She was strangely calm. Her emotional buffeting with Callan, Annette and Mrs Bennett all in such a short space of time, and so recently, had left her numb. A few months ago she would have been adamant that she would never cross the threshold of this house, nor speak to its occupants. And now here she was about to see a man she hadn't seen for three years, who had once been the love of her life.

Did love linger like the ember of a fire? When she saw Matthew, would the ember be fanned into life once more? The door opened.

'Kate. How lovely. Come in, please,' Moyra said, already moving forward awkwardly to take Kate's coat and scarf.

There wasn't room in the narrow hall for two people so Moyra retreated, allowing Kate to enter. There was a smell of fresh paint and the walls and woodwork were bright and gleaming; not a mark or a scuff in sight. It was a far cry from Invermalloch House, where signs of age, long term usage and downright deterioration were abundant.

She followed Moyra into the living room where a maroon sofa and armchairs swallowed up the space. Behind, at the windows were paler chintz curtains and one brass standard lamp graced the furthest corner. There was no room for anything else.

'Please take a seat,' Moyra said rather formally.

Kate could hear coughing in another room. Moyra frowned in concern then quickly smiled at Kate.

'Matthew's still got that horrible cold I told you about. It's why he missed the Spring Festival, which was a shame; I know he was hoping to see you.'

Her fingers plucked at the knitted

tassels on her long cardigan as she spoke. Moyra's eyes continually darted to Kate's and away again, seeking perhaps reassurance of what she was saying.

'Gosh, here I am gabbling away and I haven't even offered you a drink,' Moyra said brightly, her fingers still active, tapping gently now on her bump which seemed to Kate to have grown in the days since the Festival. Presumably that was normal.

How would I know? Kate thought and was surprised by the sharp pang that brought. Did Callan want children? He would make a great father. He could show the children how to look after animals and how to heal them; how to mend a broken wing or plaster a pet dog's leg. He had patience and good humour in bucketfuls, much more than Kate had. Just what their offspring would need for a happy upbringing.

Their offspring? Even if Callan did want a family one day, did he want it with her? Annette's unwelcome image popped up before her mind's eye. Despite Kate's decision to trust Callan and his protestations of love for her, she could not rid herself of the notion that Annette was in some way still on the scene. It was possible, after all, to love two people. Callan could still harbour passion for Annette whether he acted on it or not. After all, wasn't Kate herself at this very moment sitting in the house of a man she had loved entirely for several years of her young life?

Another cough brought her back to her surroundings. Moyra had gone to get drinks. There was a clattering of plates and a kettle singing harshly somewhere. But now, in the doorway, stood Matthew.

Kate rose slowly. She had forgotten how thin he was. She had always liked that about him. His mild stoop of the shoulders and narrow frame gave him the impression of professorial intent. Here was a man, it said, who spent much time hunched over books learning complicated facts. The owlish glasses, very John Lennon, completed the look.

'Kate,' he said simply, blinking at her.

At that moment Moyra arrived with a dainty tray of cups and cake and for a second they were framed together in Kate's vision, the tall young man and his plump, homely wife.

Matthew briefly stroked Moyra's hair as she passed to the small table to lay the tray. She smiled back at him and was transformed in that instant from homely to beautiful. Love shone from her brown eyes and that was all that was needed to lift her from plain to something quite different. Kate was outside that magic circle during the brief exchange.

Then it broke apart as all three sat and took coffee and crumbly home-made carrot cake. Kate was glad of the distraction.

'We're so glad you agreed to come and visit us,' Matthew said finally, after they had all sampled the baking and made suitably appreciative noises.

'So glad,' echoed Moyra.

'We've tried before to contact you through your mum,' Matthew said.

Kate had the grace to blush faintly. 'She did pass on each message. You mustn't blame my mother. She's spent the last three years trying to persuade me to meet you.'

'We can understand why you didn't want to.' It was Moyra's turn to blush. She pulled at the cardigan's tassels until Matthew gently lifted her hand and clasped it in his own.

'We couldn't help it, Kate,' he said bluntly. 'I thought I loved you. I wasn't being dishonest. But in a way we grew up together, didn't we, in those college years? We mistook friendship and compatibility for romantic love. Or at least, I did. And Moyra was there the whole time. One day it hit me like a bomb blast; that what I felt for her was so completely different. I was truly in love for the first time. I couldn't believe it when Moyra said she felt the same way about me. I was flabbergasted!'

'I knew how I felt about Matthew from the moment you introduced me to him. It was love at first sight for me. It sounds corny, doesn't it?' Moyra said. 'But do you know why that phrase exists? Because it's true. It really happens to people. Do you remember when we met?'

Kate cast her mind back. It all seemed so very long ago that it could have happened to someone else. In a way, it had. Kate was not the naïve, trusting young girl who had enrolled at college to study librarianship anymore. She was older, wiser, battered and bruised by experience.

'Was it Cath Healey's twenty-first birthday party?' she hazarded a guess.

There had been so many parties and fun get-togethers and each one had memories of Matthew and Moyra attached. Which was why she never dusted down those memories and replayed them. Not ever.

'Yes, it was. Remember Cath hired that hotel function suite and it was a

159

Hawaiian night? Gosh, she was lucky her daddy was so rich. That must have cost an absolute fortune.'

'I do remember,' Kate agreed. 'The rest of us were gobsmacked by the flowers and cocktails and all the specially laid-on waiting staff. It was like another world to us.'

Moyra giggled. 'We had made our own wonky grass skirts.'

'Sewing was never my strong point.' Kate grinned.

They had worn the grass strands over pink voile and both had high-heeled strappy sandals that were most unlikely Hawaiian garb.

'We had a lot of fun in those days together,' Moyra added wistfully. She looked at Kate. 'I miss you, miss our friendship. I know I messed up but I never meant to hurt you. I just couldn't hide my feelings for Matthew any longer. And when he told me he loved me . . . well suffice it to say I'll never reach a moment of pure happiness quite like it ever again!'

'I miss our friendship too. I've closed people out for so long. But it is lonely without close friends,' Kate said carefully.

Moyra got up unsteadily with Matthew's help and Kate rose to meet her hug. Her eyes were streaming. Between them was the heat of Moyra's taut, round stomach.

'Someone's butting in,' Kate joked, wiping away her tears.

Moyra patted her tummy. 'He already wants Mummy's attention at all times. The nausea is gone, thank goodness, but now I'm sure I can feel tiny kicks like little bubbles rising.'

Kate turned to Matthew. He was watching his wife tenderly. It was clear that here was a love that not only would last a lifetime but was big enough and generous enough to include a baby or two because their love would expand as much as was required for family life. And looking at Matthew, Kate realised that she felt no passion for him.

Instead she found herself comparing

161

him with Callan almost involuntarily. Callan's dark, rugged good looks compared to Matthew's pale, receding hair and thin shoulders. Callan's broad-shouldered outdoor lifestyle compared to Matthew's intellectual aura.

'I wish you both the best,' Kate said, and meant it wholeheartedly. She moved to embrace Matthew as a friend and felt nothing but friendship.

'We do have one request to make of you,' Moyra said. She glanced at her husband. Matthew nodded. 'We would love you to be Godmother to our baby when he or she is born.'

Having felt she could feel no more emotion, Kate now was shaken by a tumult of love and affection for these two people. She could hardly form words to thank them.

'It comes with responsibility,' Moyra told her, mock sternly.

'I'm scared now. What do I have to do?'

'You have to visit us often. Later on, you have to take him or her out to play and of course spoil them rotten until I complain to you!'

'I think I can manage all that. I'll certainly try.'

Kate hugged them both again and accepted a large paper hanky from Matthew so she could dry her eyes yet again.

She left them waving at the front door of the bungalow and, exhausted but happy, drove away, determined to rekindle all of what had once been into a brand new phase of friendship.

12

Mrs Sheffield had a priority listing when it came to her children. Lately Josh was priority one — but it wasn't always that way. The list was not about love. She loved all four of them equally. No, the list was a measure of how much worry she felt about them.

Before Mr Sheffield had passed away, it was fair to say that Melissa had held top position on this list for years. Her flamboyant nature and complete lack of propriety often landed her in hot water. Once she discovered boys, pubs and freedom, she was never far from her mother's mind.

In those days Jenny and Josh had switched at regular intervals between number two and number three placings as a result of illnesses, fall-outs with friends or exam results. Nothing major, thank goodness. Josh had been such a happy child, ready to go with the flow. He had a great bunch of friends and later played saxophone in an amateur jazz band. It made it all the more painful now that he had vanished onto the dangerous streets of London with nothing but his saxophone and a kitbag of clothes.

But Kate had never worried her mother. She had always held the lowest number four spot. She was calm and unruffled, self-contained. Even that awful business with her fiancé Matthew and best friend Moyra had not sent her off-balance. She had quietly gone on with her life and had not been affected by it as far as Mrs Sheffield could see.

But Kate was worrying her now. The text message from Jenny was alarming. She had met Kate for coffee yesterday. The text was simple: *Need to rally round. Organise Gran's birthday. Kate not possible.*

Kate not possible. What was not possible? Blast these modern communications! It made no sense. She would have to speak to Jenny.

The worry had admittedly started when Kate had decided out of the blue to go and live in the old house in the wilds of Argyll. It was as if something had snapped in her. Not that she was any less calm, but it was nevertheless a strange thing to do. Then she had met that gorgeous man Callan Jamieson. For a while Kate looked so content. Now he, like Josh, had gone missing and Kate was 'not possible'.

Mrs Sheffield looked again at her youngest daughter's text message. *Rally round*. Kate was always ready to help the family, now it was time for the family to help her. Mrs Sheffield picked up the phone and began to dial.

★ ★ ★

Jenny turned up unexpectedly at Invermalloch House the previous day. She'd taken her bike on the train from Glasgow and cycled the last part along snowy roads, with brown slush spraying up from the passing cars and icy hail flinging down from the heavens. Despite that it was exhilarating, the power of her legs pushing her along, the fresh stinging air whipping up colour in her cheeks and the capacity of her lungs increasing until she felt she was eating the oxygen as she flew along.

Her backpack contained energy bars to sustain her. It was getting easier, the eating. The bars were small but sufficient to boost her and she combined them with thick vegetable broth from a food flask. Her muscles and tendons felt strengthened from the past weeks of training and her skin practically glowed. Chris had been a brilliant coach on all things cycling. She could replace a wheel, fix a puncture and carry out basic maintenance checks. All were essential skills if she and Heidi were to make their journey safely across India. She slowed to take the turn into the lane at Invermalloch House.

The old house was sombre and gloomy in the shadows. Jenny shivered.

She would hate living so far from the City. Why did Kate move out here?

'Jenny! What on earth are you doing here?' Kate demanded when she opened the front door.

'That's a nice welcome,' Jenny teased.

'No, no. I just didn't expect you. Come on in.'

'Is Callan here?'

There was a pause. Then Kate said, 'No. He's gone back to Ireland.'

'Oh.' Jenny was lost for words momentarily. 'I thought . . . '

'Thought what? That he and I were together? So did I. But now, I don't know what to think. I haven't heard from him at all. He told me he loved me but . . . ' Kate shrugged helplessly.

'Should you be concerned? Has something happened to him?'

'No. He's still in contact with his friend Annette. I met her yesterday in the village and she was keen to tell me how happy he is back in Connemara.'

'Aren't you going to fight for him?'

Jenny asked fiercely.

Kate looked at Jenny in astonishment. Then she burst out laughing.

Jenny laughed too. 'Sorry, that did sound a bit mediaeval.'

'Just slightly. I had a sudden mental image of me and Annette wrestling in the village square.'

'Still it wouldn't do any harm to write to him — or even visit.'

'I've thought about it,' admitted Kate. 'Once Gran's birthday is over, I might just fly to Ireland and get an answer once and for all.'

Talking of Gran's birthday ... ' Jenny's words tailed away as she looked around at Invermalloch House's bare walls and complete lack of tidiness. There were no fresh flowers or scent of wood polish or any sign of a welcome — just the usual jumble of stuff.

'Yes. It's only a few days away. I just can't summon up any enthusiasm for it. I miss Callan; I miss Josh and I miss Dad. But I do want Gran to be happy. It's a special occasion and I so want to make it really good for her.'

Jenny nodded. She missed their dad, too. She'd have loved him to see her so proficient at her cycling and for him to listen to her plans for her journey to India. Talking to Mum just wasn't the same; she worried too much and it took the excitement right out of everything.

'It's very quiet. Where are the animals?'

Kate sighed. 'That's one thing I have managed to do. I've disbanded the rescue centre. The crow was ready to be released anyway. I've found a good home for Gilly the goat on the farm up the way. As for the baby hedgehogs, David Connaughie next door begged me for the chance to care for them.'

'I thought his mother was an ogre?'

'Jenny! She's actually pleasant to me now when I meet her, since I'm no longer a scarlet woman ready to snatch her husband.'

They both laughed again.

Kate made a cafetiere of good Columbian coffee and located a few

forlorn biscuits and they settled themselves in the kitchen by the fire. Kate
looked properly at Jenny with a
scrutinising eye.

'You're different. Have you actually
put on weight, little sister?'

Jenny flushed prettily. 'I'm feeling
hungry again,' she confessed, pleased
that Kate had noticed. 'All the cycling
is building me up, too. I'm determined
to go to India with Heidi. I've organised
a gap year so I have my college place to
go back to.'

This was said with an edge of
defiance. Jenny was growing up, but she
was still the Sheffield baby after all. She
fully expected Kate to still disapprove,
but Kate merely nodded mildly.

'Don't you want to echo what Mum's
saying? *You've no idea how dangerous
India is; if you don't get murdered in
the overcrowded cities then you're
going to catch cholera and die in an
under-equipped field hospital.*'

'I've had to do a bit of growing up
myself in the last day or so. I did agree

171

with Mum originally, as you know. When I found out your plan, I thought you were mad, but now I think you're right to go.' She smiled encouragingly at her sister. 'Travel will be good for you; you'll meet new people and spread your wings without your older siblings telling you what to do. It's very sensible to keep your college place open. If you don't want it in a year's time then you can rethink at that point.'

Jenny's mouth dropped open. 'Wow. I wanted your blessing, Kate but this is miles better — thank you! I'll blog every day, I promise, so you know where I am and what I'm up to.'

'I look forward to it.'

'Of course Melissa's having kittens trying to fit all her clothes into one bag. Can you imagine?'

'Why would she do that? Is she going on holiday?'

Jenny put her hand over her mouth in surprise. 'You don't know? Melissa's coming too.'

'Cycling across India? Now you really

are mad. Liss's never been on a bike in her life! She hates exercise.'

'Ahh, but Chris is a fitness fanatic so if she wants to keep him then she has to take up sport.'

'I thought you and Chris . . . ' Kate started, bewildered. She was beginning to empathise with her mother who was in a state of continual perplexity over the antics of her children. Usually there was more logic to the antics, though.

'I like Chris a lot. And yes, I probably fancied him when I met him. He's very good-looking. But he's kinda old for me. Once he got teaching me cycling it was more like a big brother thing going on, you know.'

'Oh,' was all Kate could manage.

'Anyway, Melissa's in seventh heaven. He's keen on her and she's besotted with him. She's even cut down on her drinking 'cos he's teetotal. Not healthy, you see. It's macrobiotics and organics all the way for him. Luckily, Chris is up for the India trip too. Four's a good number for travelling. It'll be great!'

Kate had trouble envisaging her lively sister cycling miles, fuelled by healthy foods and no booze, but it had to be better for her. Maybe she was getting back on track alongside Jenny.

Kate herself was still derailed — and Josh wasn't even anywhere near the track, to complete her confused metaphor.

'And so now we need to sort you out,' Jenny told her brightly, as if she had heard Kate's thoughts.

'Don't fret about Gran's party. Buy your gifts and leave the rest to me.'

★   ★   ★

Loch Malloch was beautiful. Its frozen surface glinted silver where the sun touched it in weak fingers through the metallic clouds. There was no one there. Who would be out so early on a frosty spring morning when there was toast and hot coffee and the radio for company? Only Kate — and she was glad of the solitude.

She wandered slowly along the brittle loch edge, watching the ice break into spidery cracks with each footstep. A stone, flipped by her shoe, clattered across the frozen surface with a satisfying, hollow resonance.

On the far shore three tufted ducks flew up, silhouetted like china ducks on a living room wall. They were supposed to bring luck, those china ducks, but Kate didn't feel lucky. Too much was still out of kilter. Perhaps she had managed to hold the ribbons of family life from slipping loose but none of them were truly back to normal yet.

Dad would have loved this place. The familiar pang of pain accompanied this spontaneous thought, and yet the pain was softer, mellowed by time. Perhaps it would never fully vanish, Kate realised. There would always be a sadness, a loss, associated with her memories of her father. That was natural. But memories, like muscles, needed to be exercised to stay usable. Just as she was making herself remember times with

Matthew and Moyra, it was time to remember Dad and family memories without that sharp grief.

He would have enjoyed walking with her at Loch Malloch. They could have argued over species of duck and beaten each other at skimming pebbles over the ice. They would have enjoyed the signs of spring she could see, such as the lambs on the far fields and the acid yellow of coltsfoot flowers dotted about in the grass.

She imagined introducing him to Callan. They would have taken to each other, she was sure. Both of them were strong characters, easy-going, outdoor types. *Callan*. Now the pang was sharp. It wasn't grief, exactly, but a mixture of love and hope and loss. Would he ever return? Was he, too, seeing new lambs in the fields around his Connemara cottage and watching as celandine and purslane returned colours to the ground? Was he mulling over his love for Kate? Or was he deciding that, in the end, that love wasn't sufficient for him to leave his beloved home for?

The mournful cry of a black-throated diver in the far marsh made her jump. Kate looked at her watch. It was time to go.

★ ★ ★

Jenny and Melissa had arrived very early armed with organic chickens, a bucket of vegetables and a bag of beautifully wrapped presents. They were the front runners of a small army. Mum and Betty were then to arrive with Gran, and of course Mrs Bennett would be there for the celebratory lunch. Chris and Nicky were also invited and, according to Melissa who was bubbling over with happiness, were bringing chocolate pudding and clotted cream from the farm.

Invermalloch House was shining with warm, yellow light. It looked so very inviting in the stark landscape. All the windows were lit up, even upstairs. Kate guessed that Melissa and Jenny had been busy making up beds for the guests, all of whom would stay the night except for Mrs Bennett. It was too hazardous a journey back to the city late on a frosty night when public transport was unpredictable at best.

Kate walked round to the back door. She greeted Gilly the goat in her shelter in the garden shed. Gilly snickered a greeting.

'And a happy day to you, silly Gilly,' Kate whispered, rubbing the goat's head where she liked it, on the coarse fur between her rough, scaly horns. 'I'll miss you; but you'll be happy on the farm. The kids there are waiting for you to play with them.'

She gently left the shed door ajar for air and shelter against the elements.

She pushed open the kitchen door and a waft of hot, fragrantly spiced air hit her nostrils, along with a sudden cacophony of noise and chatter.

Melissa and Jenny were shouting at each other across a huge, black roasting tin holding two half-cooked crispy brown monster chickens. The range door was open blasting out heat while both girls were red in the face, brandishing spoons and a food thermometer.

At the sink, Betty and Mrs Sheffield were peeling potatoes and shelling peas at a vast rate of knots. Years of experience were showing. Gran was ensconced in the blue armchair, her elderly, shaking hands carefully folding napkins into bishops' hats for tucking into wine glasses at the dinner table.

A swinging jazz beat from Gran's radio competed with the chat, the sizzle of cooking chicken juices and the rush of the cold tap as the vegetables were rinsed.

Mrs Sheffield turned and smiled at her eldest daughter. There was a sheen to her eyes as she said 'I wish Dad was here to enjoy this, Kate. I really do. He would have loved all this commotion, wouldn't he?'

'He would've been in the thick of it,' Kate agreed, giving her mum a hug.

'Remember the time Dad went for a constitutional walk before Gran's eightieth birthday lunch and was late back?' piped up Jenny as she slid the chickens back into the old oven and slammed the range door shut.

'You were so livid, Mum, I thought Dad was going to wear the meal that year,' Melissa chimed in cheekily.

Mrs Sheffield chuckled. 'And when he finally got back,' she said, enjoying the retelling of the family tale, 'he had brought us each a daffodil.'

She scrubbed furiously at a potato, then sighed and put it aside. Betty tactfully removed the rest. They were ready to roast alongside chipolata sausages and asparagus now.

'He loved his walks, that man,' Kate's mother said fondly.

'Well, Sheila dear, it's a good thing you've finally joined our rambling group. John would be glad of that,' Betty said cheerfully.

'It's thanks to Kate that I did. She kept on at me until I realised it was less bother to go along than listen to another lecture on why it was good for me!'

'Oh, but Mum, I . . . '

'I'm only teasing, my love. You've done me good. You've looked after me since Dad died and I'm grateful.'

'So am I,' Jenny said unexpectedly. 'It was Kate's idea that I take a gap year from college rather than toss in the towel altogether. And if it wasn't for Kate and Callan I never would have met Chris and got so good at cycling.'

'And I wouldn't have met Chris and fallen in love,' reminded Melissa.

They all laughed.

'Let's raise our glasses — or rather our tea mugs — to Kate,' Jenny suggested cheerfully.

'To Kate,' they said together, Gran and Betty joining in.

'Oh, stop it,' Kate cried. 'I love you all but you're embarrassing me. It's Gran's special day, not mine, so let's wish Gran a very happy birthday!'

They raised their mugs, happily

chorusing a birthday greeting to the elder Mrs Sheffield who was loving every minute of it.

Then they laughed again and busied themselves once more.

In the midst of the activity Melissa managed to whisper to Kate, 'Don't think I've forgotten how you saved me from that awful man after Amy's party because I haven't. I don't know what we would do without you, Kate, to look after us all. So thank you.'

Then she hurried off after Jenny, who was draped in a linen tablecloth and pink runner and holding bags of small goodies for the table.

'Oh, there's organic fruit wine, too,' she threw back over her shoulder, with a twinkle in her eye, 'So tell me when Chris arrives!'

* * *

An hour later the dining room table was set and ready, laden with dishes and crystal so that there was no space for any more. Mats and trivets stood ready for the hot food. The bright pink napkins and gold wrapped chocolates of the centrepiece decoration made it perfect for a special party.

The side cabinet displayed cards from family and friends and in the corner stood a short but sturdy pile of gifts in intriguing shapes and sizes.

Kate looked around at her mother, sisters and Gran and Betty. Everyone looked pleased with the results. The smell of roast chicken was tantalising from the kitchen, mingling with the sweet nostalgic scents of the chocolates and the candles. Then the door bell rang.

'That'll be Mrs Bennett,' said Mrs Sheffield. 'I'll get it.'

They heard her heels click across the hall floor and the sound of the front door opening with its familiar wooden creak. Then there was a strange silence. Kate frowned at her sisters. What was her mother doing? Why was there no sound of greetings?

She went through to the hall and stopped dead. Josh was standing at the front door. A few stray snowflakes drifted in on the breeze behind him. Mrs Sheffield was motionless, hands to her mouth in disbelief. Then even as Kate appeared she was moving forward to grasp her son, soundlessly.

Kate ran too. It was Josh! It was really him! He was thinner and sported a straggly beard and long hair, but he was here. He had made it home for Gran's special birthday.

He moved into his mother's embrace and Kate saw that behind him, on the doorstep, there was someone else standing there. A tall, dark man, so sweetly familiar to her that she felt suspended in time for a moment. Then it was Kate's turn to rush. She ran to Callan and held him with such intensity that she could feel his heartbeat as she laid her head on his chest.

'Kate,' he murmured. 'My lovely Kate.'

She turned her face to his and let the warmth of his lips melt her heart.

Then, suddenly, all around them were people.

Gran, Melissa and Jenny were with Josh. Chris and Nicky arrived at the same time as Mrs Bennett and coats were handed over, gifts carried in with the chill air and they all moved to the dining room for drinks.

Mrs Bennett took a long moment to wish Kate's gran a happy birthday, her eyes sending a silent message to Kate which Kate understood perfectly.

'Here you are, pet, a gift from the Connaughies,' Mrs Bennett said, reaching into a huge raffia bag and pulling out a brown paper package.

Kate opened it, mystified. Inside was the picture she had admired that day at the Spring Festival of Invermalloch Bay.

'Davey's chuffed with getting the hedgehogs, Sally says. She's relieved he's found an outlet for all that boyish energy. He's a lovely lad but he drives her potty with his schemes. This must be her way of saying thank you.'

'It's a wonderful painting,' Kate said.

'Looks like I'm finally accepted in Invermalloch just as I'm about to leave.'

'Maybe you should stay — only without the centre,' Mrs Bennett added.

Kate laughed. Mrs Sheffield appeared and took Mrs Bennett off to the dining room to join the others.

Callan and Kate were left discreetly, still wrapped in each other's arms. Eventually Kate stood back from him a little, still holding his hand as though to prevent him from once more disappearing.

'Where have you been? Why did you leave me?'

'Leave you? Never that.' Callan's Irish lilt was tender. 'We parted on an argument that's true but I told you I loved you and I said I would be back.'

'But then you went home to Connemara.'

'Connemara! Who told you that? No, I went to London to find your brother. I knew you would never be truly happy until you'd sorted out your family and helped them. In turn I knew I could help you by finding Josh and persuading him to come home.

'I started with the address in Hackney, spoke to squatters and people who'd met him and I managed eventually to track him down. To be honest, I think he was ready to come home. I was just the catalyst.'

Callan stroked Kate's hair in a gesture so intimate she shivered with joy.

'Why didn't you phone me?' he demanded roughly, his fingers twining in her hair as he kissed her hungrily.

'Why didn't you phone me?' Kate echoed weakly, between kisses.

He pulled away from her, puzzled.

'Did you not read my letter? I left it at my cottage with Annette for her to give to you, when I decided to travel to London. I said in it that I wouldn't phone you in case you got your hopes up that I had found Josh each time I called. Instead, I asked you to phone me from time to time and I left my new mobile number.'

'I never got your letter,' Kate told him. 'I went to the cottage to tell you that I was in love with you, but Annette told me you'd gone back to Ireland.'

Callan shook his head ruefully. 'That woman. The leopard doesn't change its spots after all. I should have known she'd be up to her tricks as usual. I thought we could be just friends, but she's still her wily self. I'm sorry, Kate. I shouldn't have entrusted the letter to her.'

Kate pulled him back into her caress. 'Forget her,' she whispered. 'It's a special birthday and you are my best present ever. Let's enjoy ourselves. It's the best revenge we can have.'

She led him through to the dining room where the celebration family meal was just beginning.

Mrs Sheffield was heaping Josh's plate high with meat and roast potatoes and spoonfuls of rich wine gravy.

Jenny was tucking in heartily to a decent helping of food, while Melissa was carefully filling her own glass and Chris's with soda before offering around wine and beer.

Mrs Bennett and Kate's gran were reminiscing about many birthday celebrations past while Betty was content to sip her drink and smile happily at everyone.

Callan surveyed the scene.

'I think your Dad would approve,' he said softly.

Kate blinked and smiled at him. 'Yes, Dad would have approved very much of his family and its friends, both old and new, celebrating together this year in this dear place.'

There was a sudden shriek and Melissa shot to her feet.

'That awful goat. It's eating the daffodils I brought for Gran!'

Sure enough, Gilly the goat had slipped her tether and butted her way into the house, where she was now munching and bleating contentedly.

'Well, it's only fair she should join us after all,' Kate laughed, 'She's part of

189

the family really.'

She snuggled closer to Callan as they sat together in the heart of the Sheffield family.

THE END

Other titles in the
Linford Romance Library:

BOHEMIAN RHAPSODY

Serenity Woods

Elfie Summers is an archaeologist
with a pet hate of private collectors.
Cue Gabriel Carter, a self-made
millionaire. He invites Elfie to
accompany him to Prague to verify
the authenticity of an Anglo-Saxon
buckle, said to grant true love to
whoever touches it. And whilst
Gabriel's sole motive is to settle an
old score, Elfie just wants to return
to her quiet, scholarly life — but the
city and the buckle have other
ideas . . .

LOVE AND CHANCE

Susan Sarapuk

When schoolteacher Megan bumps into a gorgeous Frenchman in the Hall of Mirrors at Versailles, she thinks she will never see him again. Until the Headteacher asks her to visit Lulu Santerre, a pupil who is threatening not to return to school. Megan discovers that Lulu's brother Raphael is the man she met at Versailles ... When Lulu goes missing Raphael and Megan are thrown together and both of them have to make decisions about their future.

WISH YOU WERE HERE?

Sheila Holroyd

Cara was hoping to spend Christmas in England with her boyfriend, but her mother sweeps her off to a holiday home in Spain. However, they are forced to stay in a hotel, wondering if they can afford the bill. There, she becomes attracted to Nick, despite his being ten years her junior. But, unexpectedly, her boyfriend, Geoff, and Nick's girlfriend, Lily, appear at the hotel. Then both Nick's and Cara's fathers add to the complicated network of relationships . . .